THE WEDDING MURDER

A CYPRUS COVE COZY MYSTERY

Liz Turner

Contents

Chapter 1
Death by Chocolate

"Can't taste a thing," Colleen stated with a dismissive wave of her dimpled hand, her pig-like nose turned up to the sky.

The offending piece of vanilla sponge, draped in fresh strawberries and cream, lay rejected with hardly a nibble missing.

"Well," came the indignant reply, "of course *you* can't. You're used to everything absolutely dripping in decadence and sugar. Whereas my palette is far more refined."

Violet Finch looked down the length of her nose at the pudgy woman opposite her, decked in a polka dot peach dress with the stitch strength being tested to the limits. Her thin lips curled into a disapproving sneer. Everything about Colleen Austin was over the top and loud.

"What you consider refined means dull in my vocabulary."

"You didn't even taste my strawberry cake!" Violet accused her, after noticing that barely a crumb was missing from the slice she had carefully prepared for Colleen's scrutiny.

"The cream smelled ever so slightly rotten," Colleen commented, her tiny eyes darting away from the offending cake.

Violet snorted in disgust at the flagrant insult so casually flung her way. She dipped a perfectly manicured finger into the cream and touched it delicately on her tongue.

"This cream is perfect. So fresh it is still warm from the cow," she declared stubbornly. "Now taste my cake!" she ordered loudly.

Colleen squinted at her and clenched her jaw with resolve. "Shan't," the woman insisted with a folding of her wobbly arms across her enormous bosom.

"I tasted your sickly death-by-chocolate cake which, I should add, not only glued my tongue to the roof of my mouth for a solid five minutes, but certainly *killed* my appetite too," she retorted. "It's only fair you taste my cake in return. You will likely find that it is an entirely pleasurable experience!"

"I can tell by looking at it that it's dry," Colleen said with a sniff, "and there's too little sugar. The texture is all wrong, and it simply doesn't smell sweet enough."

"That's because your pile of diabetic's death is overpowering the free air with a pungent, sickly-sweet stench that is attracting every rabid critter in a fifty-mile radius," Violet declared tartly, her cheeks reddening from the passion with which she delivered the words.

"How dare you!" Colleen hissed at her, her piggy eyes narrowing. Her face rapidly transformed from sweet serenity into a shade of violent crimson. "My death-by-chocolate cake is absolutely exquisite and just happens to be Isabel's favorite!"

"I highly doubt that," Violet scoffed with disbelief. "Isabel is a charming young lady, who has an artistic eye and a rather subtle sense of style, which I adore. Your domineering overtures have eclipsed her taste for far too long."

Colleen blinked at Violet a few times, her plump lips reforming the unfamiliar words she had just been bombarded by. She had no idea what they meant, but she knew she wanted to wipe the self-satisfied smirk off Violet's perfectly made-up face.

"Don't you dare tell me what's what when it comes to my Isabel," Colleen growled at her with almost feral hostility. "She is *my* daughter after all."

"Taste the cake," Violet ordered her, her jaw clenching in between each word she hissed out. "*My* future daughter-in-law would want you to."

Colleen pursed her lips and folded her arms stubbornly across her chest with deliberate defiance.

Violet shook her head as though she refused to accept Colleen's ridiculous rejection. With a trembling hand that appeared to act of its own accord, she raised the silver cake fork and carefully poked the prongs into the soft sponge of the cake. She lifted a large chunk, with a generous dab of cream and piece of strawberry, admiring her skillful work for a moment, before taking the piece between two fingers and shoving it into Colleen's mouth.

Colleen choked and spluttered bits of cream and cake crumbs everywhere. Violet found this hilarious, and she chortled a ladylike tinkle while wiping her hands clean on a napkin.

"You see, it's delicious. Admit it," Violet insisted as she touched a cotton handkerchief to the corner of each eye to wipe away the tears.

Colleen was most certainly not going to admit it, even though the cream was perfectly fresh, and the tang of sweet strawberry danced across her taste buds, only to be cushioned by a delicate vanilla sponge.

"Revolting!" Colleen declared in a high-pitched squeal, though she had swallowed most of the taster forced upon her. "How dare you assault me like that!"

"Oh, don't be so dramatic," Violet chided with an uncomfortable laugh. "I merely encouraged you to sample a small portion of -"

Violet was interrupted by a wad of chocolate cake that slammed into the front bodice of her gorgeous, white A-frame dress. Dollops of chocolate ganache dropped down onto her shoes as Violet tried to scoop the brown mess off her chest.

Colleen snorted like a pig as she watched the furious Violet end up with an impossibly large stain stretch across her bosom. Her laughter caught in her throat as something cold and wet slapped against her cheek. The definite smell of chocolate revealed the make-up of the substance. Colleen looked down and realized she had been hit with several blobs of her own chocolate cake, adding a series of dark brown polka dots to the white ones on her peach dress.

"You've ruined my dress!" Colleen screeched at her as she danced about and flicked bits of cake off herself.

"You attacked my dress first!" Violet shot back. "At least my addition of stains to your dress actually improved the overall look."

Colleen reached for the remainder of the strawberry cream cake, clawing her fingers through the cloud of cream and aggressively ripping out a chunk. She held it up into the air and let out a rage-filled shriek, before hurling the clod of cake at Violet.

Most of the cream cake slapped into Violet's face. She howled with fury and blindly reached for any remnant of cake she could lay her hands on.

"Mom…" Isabel stammered as cream flew past her shoulder and slapped into the wall. "What's going on in here?"

The women froze, arms outstretched and hands holding chunks of cake, poised mid-air and ready to launch cake and frosting at each other.

"Izzie, darling," Colleen droned. "We were trying to decide on the best cake for your wedding."

"By hurling it at each other?" Isabel asked with confusion. "Look at my kitchen!"

The tiny loft kitchen was covered in cake debris, which Isabel's three cats had encroached on and were blissfully licking up.

"Tinkles is already diabetic after just two weeks of you being here, Mom," Isabel added. She groaned under the weight of her heftiest cat as she hoisted him into her arms, his chocolate coated tongue still dangling out the side of his mouth.

"This was entirely my fault," Violet began humbly, a chocolate coated hand on her stained chest. "I was annoyed that Colleen refused to taste my cake after I tasted hers."

Isabel turned to give her retreating mother a stern look.

"Yes," Colleen admitted meekly, "that is partially true. I didn't want to taste her cake, but only because," she sniffed and dabbed away a tear, "I wanted my daughter to have *my* special cake be a part of her wedding day!"

Colleen began howling into a frilly handkerchief while Isabel summoned the strength to deal with her emotionally taxing mother. The only thing worse than the dominant overbearing version of Colleen was the sobbing, yet equally manipulative, version.

"Alright, then we can go with the death-by-chocolate cake," Isabel surrendered, as she had done so many times when it came to her wedding.

Violet let out a sniff and soon her handkerchief was also out, blotting away rouge-colored make-up.

"What's wrong?" Isabel asked with concern, a hand on her future mother-in-law's sticky arm.

"It's just I don't have a daughter of my own," she cried, "and seeing Ricardo marry you has made me the happiest woman alive, because now I have you as my very own daughter."

"That makes me happy too," Isabel consoled her, "so why the tears?"

"I'll never have another wedding to be a part of, and I would desperately love my cake to be an important feature of your wedding too!" she howled into Isabel's shoulder, her face leaving a brown patch on Isabel's sleeve.

"I have an idea," Isabel conceded with a heavy sigh. "Why don't we have both a strawberry cream cake and a death-by-chocolate cake? That way I can enjoy making both of you happy on my wedding day."

Colleen and Violet's sobs subsided as they turned tear-stained, yet hopeful, faces to look at her.

"Do you really mean that?" Colleen asked in her mastered little girl voice.

"Why not," Isabel said, feigning a smile. "Everyone loves cake."

Milly, her favorite and most perceptive cat, hopped into her arms from the counter. Isabel clutched her close, Milly's grey fur brushing against her cheek. At least Milly could sense Isabel's anxiety and discomfort brewing beneath the surface, even if her own family could not.

"Now, I came to do a final fitting of the dress you've both been working on," Isabel said with another forced smile. "It is finished, right?"

"Yes, darling, of course. Your mother would never still be busy with your wedding dress the day before the wedding," Violet assured her. "Let us just wash up quickly and then we can try on your dress."

"Thanks," Isabel gushed with relief. "I hadn't heard from either of you all morning, so I was beginning to panic."

"I think you'll love it, dear," Violet said with a reassuring smile. "It was hard to decide what would work best for your petite figure, but we settled on a design. Your mother decided she needed to add some embellishments to make it a little more... unique," she added stiffly.

"I can't wait," Isabel lied, a feeling of dread sinking into the pit of her stomach. Milly gave her cheek a sandpapery lick that was meant to offer comfort.

The truth was the dress, along with everything else, had been one enormous fight between her mother and her mother-in-law to be. She was sure her wedding was going to result in a dead body, if not two.

Isabel Austin trudged downstairs and into her art studio. Since her family had descended on her for the wedding, there were few places Isabel felt at ease. Her art studio provided a quiet sanctuary, especially since it contained storage cupboards large enough for her to hide inside. Her cats usually gave her away. The three of them would sniff her out and sit and meow outside the door she was hiding behind, leading Colleen Austin straight to her missing daughter.

"I know it'll all be over soon, Milly," Isabel whispered to her cat, "but I'm not sure I can last much longer."

Milly meowed and Harry worked his sleek body between her legs, his silky, black tail swishing against her skin.

"Thank you, Harry, I knew you'd see things from my point of view. Then again, you were always terrified of my mother too."

Tinkles let out a fat meow which Isabel interpreted to mean that he was quite content with Colleen's visit, as it meant there was plenty of pie and cake around for him to gorge on when no one was looking.

"Yes, well, you're only loyal to food, Tinkles. And once the family leaves, and the wedding is over, you're going on a strict diet, and I mean it this time," Isabel informed her third cat, though she already felt her heart give way at the thought of starving her beloved boy. He could make his head look so skinny when he was on diet.

Tinkles turned his enormous tortoise shell back on her and let out a sulky hiss of disapproval.

"Talking to your cats again," a friendly voice sounded from the direction of the entrance.

Isabel spun on her heel and discovered her very first art student, Rosemary, poking her head through the door and offering a sympathetic smile.

"I came to see if you were still surviving the pre-wedding madness, but judging by the conversation I just overheard, I came just in time," Rosemary said with a warmhearted chuckle.

Isabel hurried to the door and threw her arms around the old woman, nearly throwing her off balance.

"I'm so glad you stopped by. Mom and Vi got into a huge fight and pelted each other with cake!" Isabel said in a low voice, her eyes darting to the flight of stairs to make sure they were not being overheard.

"Oh dear," Rosemary shook her head. "That is a bit of a disaster. Did you tell them you wanted chocolate eclairs for your wedding cake?"

Isabel chewed on her lip and smiled weakly, her face crumpling into helpless defeat.

"I couldn't," Isabel exploded as she stomped away, her feet echoing on the old floorboards that creaked under her pacing.

Rosemary saw herself in the little studio kitchen and switched the overused coffee machine on. It began gurgling away, spitting occasionally, and churning out the sound of grating gears.

"Isabel!" a shrill voice sounded from the top of the stairs.

Isabel jolted in fright and then meekly called back, "Yes?"

"Brides do not stomp!" her mother informed her. "They glide down the aisle."

"Sorry," Isabel called back, her face darkening as she turned back to Rosemary. "You see what I mean? I can't do anything in my own house, let alone choose what *I* want for my own wedding."

"So, you chose one of their cakes, then?" Rosemary asked.

She handed Isabel a steaming cup of java.

"Not quite," Isabel replied with a guilty smile. "They just both looked so sad and rejected, and I didn't want to disappoint either of them, so we're having both."

"Come here," Rosemary ordered, after setting their coffee down again. She enfolded Isabel gently in her arms and instructed her to breathe in and out until she had calmed down. "There, feel any better?"

"A little," Isabel smiled feebly and guzzled down the strong coffee, trying to suck as much strength from it as she could. "I'm waiting to do a dress fitting."

"I thought you had your eye on a wedding dress in town?"

"I did," Isabel admitted in a barely audible whisper, "but then Colleen and Violet thought they could create something better."

Rosemary's dark eyebrow spiked, and her eyes widened with disbelief. "You let them make your dress?" she muttered in horror. "Can your mother even sew?"

"She knows her way around a sewing machine, but she's finished nothing." Isabel paused and broke into a fresh wave of tears. "I didn't know what to do, and I didn't want to hurt them!" Isabel wailed.

The door at the top of the stairs creaked open again, and another voice bellowed, "Isabel darling, brides don't wail either. It's unbecoming."

Isabel looked as though she was going to do more than just wail. Rosemary gave her a warning frown and a squeeze of the hand for extra strength.

"Yes, mom-Vi," Isabel replied graciously, in a shaky voice.

"We'll be ready for you in another ten minutes," Violet called down.

Isabel sighed and sank her face into her hands.

"Have you talked to Ricardo about this?" Rosemary asked in a low voice.

Isabel thought of the handsome, sweet, and intelligent man who was to be her groom. He was understanding and sensitive to her feelings, but even he had bolted with his tail between his legs when the 'mothers' had arrived. Ricardo had swamped himself in a million police cases, that all required his immediate investigation, just so that it would spare him the unbearable torture of selecting wedding décor and sampling cake.

"Ricardo kindly told me it's my wedding and I need to stand up for what I want," Isabel explained with a slight edge to her voice.

"And then he ran away as fast as he could?" Rosemary guessed.

Isabel's look provided the answer to her question.

"Izzie, darling," Rosemary began with a smile, "I didn't just stop by to see how you were doing."

"Oh?"

"Remember I told you I wanted to bring Micky as a date to the wedding?"

"Yes, and then he ditched you for a sailing trip with his old buddies," Isabel recalled.

"Well, he surprised me by docking here this morning!" Rosemary explained with a delighted smile.

"I see," Isabel nodded slowly.

"I know it's last minute, and you have a hundred more important things to deal with. But is there any way you could spare an extra seat for old Micky? I do hate to attend these things on my own, especially at my age, where no one really cares about you and you just plop onto a chair like a really ancient wallflower."

"First, you're the liveliest old person I know, with a remarkable sense of humor, incredible painting skills, and the sweetest smile for twenty miles round. Second, of course Micky can come. You don't even need to ask. I do, however, have one concern," Isabel added in a more serious tone.

"What is it?" Rosemary asked, her eyes wide again.

"Are you sure this Micky guy is good for you?"

"He's the best thing that's ever happened to me. Well, second best, after starting art classes with you. Why do you ask?"

"I just have a feeling," Isabel replied reluctantly.

"Oh, no," Rosemary waved her hands in panic. "Stay away with those hunches of yours."

"What do you mean?"

"Whenever you have a bad feeling about something, someone usually ends up dead!"

"That's not true!" Isabel protested.

"That detective brain of yours seems to conjure up cases where there are none!"

"Rose," Isabel placed a comforting hand on her arm, "you're being paranoid. I was just asking because we don't really know much about Micky. He arrived in town on his boat one summer, moved into the old age village and flirted with every woman there."

"Yes, but he settled on me," Rosemary muttered defensively.

"Of course he did," Isabel agreed, "but I just want you to be careful before your heart gets too involved."

Rosemary patted her hand and nodded. "My girl, when you've lived and loved as long as I have, you learn to smell out the rats from a mile away."

"I hope so, because Micky could definitely improve in the aftershave department," Isabel mumbled.

"He cleans up well when he needs to," Rosemary moaned, "besides, there's limited fresh water available on his boat."

"Isabel!"

Isabel cringed as the sound of her name reverberated through the floorboards and sent Harry skittering across the studio floor.

"I'm being summoned. I'll see you and your handsome date tomorrow at the wedding," Isabel said with a nervous smile.

Chapter 2
Death by Cats

Rosemary's words of comfort and encouragement were drowned out by a second bellowed, beckoning from upstairs. Isabel scampered up the staircase with three inquisitive cats trailing behind her and hoping the rush was to feed them.

"We've been waiting for ages, Iz," her mother scolded her with one of her fake smiles fixed in place. "Come along."

They hoisted her up onto a little platform and then stripped off her t-shirt and shorts.

"Mom! Could I at least undress with some privacy?" Isabel begged, her hands clutching over her holey undies. She had been saving all her good pairs for when she was a married woman and actually had someone to see her underclothes.

"Oh, stop fussing," her mother snorted. "You need to get used to being seen in far less."

Violet giggled and soon both women, despite being sworn enemies, were mutually bonded by laughing at Isabel.

Her mother heaved the dress over Isabel's head and was attempting to lower it onto her. Isabel squeaked and squawked as a hundred pins scraped along her bare flesh.

"Oh, quit squirming, you little worm," her mother moaned at her.

"I thought the dress was finished," came the muffled reply from inside the heavy folds of shiny, white satin.

"It is finished, it just needs some adjustment, because -"

"I feel like I can't breathe," Isabel gasped as her fingers tried to stretch out the unrelenting fabric that acted like a vice grip around her ribs.

"That's because you visit the town bakery at least twice a day, and that's in between the enormous meals you've been scoffing down," her mother chastised her.

"Jeez, Mom, I'm stressed about the wedding and eating is how I get over it," Isabel complained.

"It's not her fault my son is a fantastic chef," Violet remarked from her armchair. "Anyway, your mother can let your dress out. What do you think of the style?"

Isabel turned and faced the floor-length mirror on her door. She was greeted with yards of ill-fitting white satin that made her look as pale as a ghost. To make matters worse, her mother had found satin in a pungent peach color and had hand stitched bulky bows out of it. To Isabel's morbid horror, Colleen had attached the enormous peach bows to the skirt of her white dress, causing parts to fold and sag under the weight. The top bodice was framed like a corset with a frilly sweetheart neckline that revealed far too much cleavage for a decent wedding. To top everything off, they covered the dress in a million pearly white sequins, which caught the light and reflected rainbows across the ceiling. Her cats were pouncing on the dazzling reflections that glittered across the floor.

Isabel's eyes filled with tears as she imagined walking down the shore to meet Ricardo in a dress she hated with the fire of a thousand suns. As decent a man as Ricardo was, he would likely plunge into the ocean and allow himself to be eaten by sharks before handing himself over for life to a woman dressed up as little Bo-peep gone hooker.

"Ah, I render my dear daughter speechless for the first time in her life. I knew she would love the bows."

"It's not quite my taste," Violet commented dryly, "but if you're happy with your mother's choice, then who am I to argue."

Isabel desperately wanted someone to argue on her behalf. She found the words 'I hate it' sticking in her throat and refusing to come out loud.

"What do you think?" her mother pressed.

"It's not what I would've chosen," Isabel managed in a strangled voice.

"Which is exactly why you love it," her mother completed her sentence for her, and Isabel felt powerless to argue.

The year she had spent living on her own and running her own life in Cyprus Cove had built up a certain amount of capability and confidence in Isabel. She had worked along with the police to solve murders and other strange cases involving art or theft. Isabel had opened and now successfully ran an art studio, which supported a wide range of skilled students from the area. Isabel had made a name for herself in Cyprus Cove and was a respected and loved member of the community.

A few weeks with her overbearing mother in town had undone all her hard work. She felt like a helpless thirteen-year-old girl, powerless to the demands of her mother. While Isabel had come to terms with how to deal with her mother, things had escalated again when Ricardo's mother, Violet, had entered the picture, and Isabel felt herself hurtling back to square one.

"I love it," Isabel squeaked, her face paling from the lack of oxygen. "I just can't breathe."

"Nonsense," her mother refused. "I think it gives you more of a waist this way. You'll just have to hold your posture correctly to enable enough airflow."

Isabel nodded mutely, ignoring the black and white spots that were dancing across her vision. Her mother's voice sounded far away, as if she were shouting over the rush of the ocean. She felt the entire world slowly slipping sideways and, after a terribly long falling sensation, Isabel closed her eyes at the sound of a loud thud.

The 'loud thud' had resulted from her head colliding with the wooden floorboards. Isabel had swooned, either from the lack of air reaching her brain, or from the sheer revulsion she felt towards the dress. She opened her eyes and discovered her body was still enrobed in the offending garment, a peach bow inches from her nose.

As her vision cleared and sound returned to normal, Isabel realized a tugging sensation around her legs. There was also an enormous amount of loud shrieking coming from the surrounding space.

"I'm alright," Isabel groaned. "Just a bump to the head."

She could feel the bruise forming on her forehead immediately. She hoped she had enough concealer to cover it for the wedding ceremony.

"Get off, you murderous beast!" came another shriek, followed by a heavy smack to her legs.

"Ouch!" Isabel complained as she sat bolt upright. "What's the deal -"

Her mother was armed with a rolling pin while Violet held up Isabel's tennis racquet. Both were circling her like she was a rabid animal that needed to be put out of her misery. But they were not looking at her. Isabel followed their gaze to a grey ball of fur that was gleefully shredding one of the peach bows. Milly and Harry could not resist the folds of fabric and reflective sequins and they had launched at Isabel's wedding dress with malevolent intent.

Isabel tried to bite back her smile as her dress shredded beneath their sharp claws, but she could not.

"Well, don't just sit their grinning!" her mother screamed at her. "Get the furry creatures off my dress!"

Isabel pulled Milly towards her and brushed her face with her hand. Milly had sequins caught in her whiskers. She did the same with Harry and vowed silently to reward each cat with some fresh fish from the market, to show her gratitude for murdering the most hideous dress Isabel had ever laid eyes on. Her cats had fought the battle for her and won.

"It's ruined!" her mother sobbed into the heaps of the torn material.

"There, there," Isabel soothed her. "I don't want any tears. I'll call the bridal store and see if they have anything in my size."

Isabel knew they had exactly the dress she really wanted, in her size, and on sale.

"Oh, no, no," her mother assured her, summoning a wicked smile, "this is nothing I can't fix."

Isabel's vision blurred, and she felt another thud as she hit the floor again.

Chapter 3
Death by Goose

Isabel peered out the window, while keeping her body hidden behind the heavy drapes. For a moment, her eyes settled on the pretty white lace that Delta had selected for her upstairs guest bedroom drapes. Isabel resisted the urge to yank the fabric off the hooks and turn it into a more suitable wedding dress than the one they had forced her into.

Delta had volunteered the use of her designer beach mansion that had more floors and rooms than the entire high school they had attended together. Delta's exotic garden gushed with scented flowers and an oasis of glowing green plants that sloped gently down to golden beach sands and turquoise waves that lapped rhythmically against the shore.

It was the most magical place to host a wedding, and it was the only element of the wedding that her mother and Violet had not violently opposed. Though Isabel had wanted the ceremony to take place on the beach by the water, they had refused, insisting that they could not expect guests to arrive at a formal occasion barefoot.

Isabel had peacefully relented, and the ceremony had been set up in the garden instead. From her elevated view,

Isabel saw some of the earlier guests arriving and finding their way to the overflowing table of lavish snacks.

Cheerful voices drifted up from the wedding guests below. Isabel spotted the famous Micky and Rosemary at the hors d'oeuvres table, with Micky shoveling as many cherry pies into his mouth as he could, while Rosey blushed and giggled apologetically at onlookers.

Violet trotted past in an all-purple outfit with a stylish pair of heels to match. She looked absolutely smashing, despite her age, and Isabel wondered how a woman of her looks and brains had stayed single for so long. Ricardo's father had walked out on them when he was just a young boy, leaving Violet to raise her son as best she could alone. Isabel marveled at the incredible job she had done, working three jobs to support Ricardo.

"There are plenty of snacks to go around, sir," Violet informed Micky reproachfully.

Micky stared at her with cherry-stained lips before his face broke out into a grin and he winked at Violet. There was a moment of awkward silence, where the pair just stared at each other, and Rosemary filled it with a tidal wave of nervous chatter. Violet shook her head and stomped off quickly while Micky turned and marched in the other direction, straight to the open bar.

Isabel's focus was redirected from this odd encounter to a loud laugh that had drawn her attention. She noticed another familiar face. Pedro, one of Ricardo's old friends, had made the trip all the way to Cyprus Cove just for the wedding. His amiable smile and striking eyes made him stand out wherever he went. Isabel noticed he was laughing outrageously at something his date had said.

"Wait, who's that?" Isabel muttered to herself, her fingers clenching the fabric of the drape.

There was a striking woman on Pedro's arm, with an alluring smile and playful eyes that wandered through the array of guests. A wave of heavy, dark hair cascaded down her back and her white cocktail dress fitted her shapely figure perfectly. Isabel wondered if the renowned bachelor, who had marked no plus one on his RSVP card, had finally abandoned his ways and selected a girl to make him an honest man.

There was another sultry laugh that was designed, and purposefully employed, to seduce whoever the owner was speaking to. Isabel had heard that laugh a million times in her art studio and it was not a laugh she had intentionally invited to her wedding.

"Debbie," Isabel hissed as she gawked at another uninvited guest from behind her safe spot.

Deborah was her painting name. But when Debbie willingly volunteered herself up to be a nude model for Isabel's drawing classes, she donned the stage name 'Bertha'. It was not exactly the name of a sex goddess, but Debbie behaved as though she was the most gorgeous woman in the room, despite being in her seventies and having had one too many facelifts.

Debbie was donned in a revealing leopard print gown that flowed out behind her like tendrils, which snatched onto any unsuspecting man that dared to look twice as she passed by.

"I didn't invite you either," Isabel murmured to herself. "It drives me insane how this is supposed to be *my* wedding, and yet I have absolutely no control over what's going on."

She slapped a hand on her forehead and recoiled at the pain that pulsated through her head. She had forgotten about the ugly bruise she had caused by falling on her face twice the day before. Isabel's pain was interrupted as her mother came into view in the garden below. Not only was she wearing a bright yellow dress that was certainly designed to outshine the bride, but she was leading a pack of geese into the garden.

Actual, live geese.

"No," Isabel gasped as she watched the fearsome birds peck at the pastries, and, sometimes, at the guests holding the pastries. "Why would you bring geese to a wedding?"

Isabel watched, mortified, as one goose waddled down the aisle, squawking most unattractively, and devouring parts of an enormous peach-colored flower arrangement. Isabel wanted to scream, but then she noticed the hideous flower arrangement.

"Peach," she hissed. "Why so much peach!"

She had specifically fought for yellow flowers. Her mother and Violet had argued that peach would liven her 'ghostly' skin tone. She should have known from the moment she set eyes on the hideous peach bows attached to her sham of a wedding dress that her mother had likely changed her flower order.

Isabel craned her neck to see what a group of tittering people were pointing at. She felt her jaw drop uncontrollably as she made eye contact with a huge ice sculpture of a family of ducks holding peach-colored balloons.

"Oh no," Isabel said as she clutched her aching chest.

She was not sure if it was the corset her mother had stitched into her ghastly wedding dress to give her a waist, or if she was hyperventilating from shock, but she was certain she was going to pass out again.

"There, there," Delta soothed her. "Here, drink this."

Delta held out a toffee-colored liquid that sparkled in the afternoon light.

"What is it?" Isabel asked as her nose crinkled from the smell.

"Whiskey, your favorite," she said, her voice dripping with sarcasm.

Delta was one of Isabel's most stunning friends. Her sleek auburn bob and striking features made her the center of attraction wherever she went. She was intelligent, wealthy, and confident, and her impeccable taste demanded respect and approval. Yet, her friend, who could have walked any runway in France, wearing top designer clothing, was confined to a revolting peach cowgirl dress, which made her look short and plump, not unlike a peach itself.

Isabel bit her lip and tried to suppress the laugh that crept up her throat.

"You know I'd do anything for you," Delta told her after downing her own three fingers of whiskey. "But this dress…"

Delta's face darkened, and she looked as though a piece of her soul had withered away and died.

"I'm a respected member of this community. I just don't know if I can show my face wearing this thing."

"I'm so sorry," Isabel apologized profusely for the third time that day. "I promise that this was not the dress I chose for you. And trust me, you look better than I do."

Delta snorted with amusement, some of the old life returning to her features. "That's not possible."

Isabel took a delicate sip of her whiskey, set her glass down, and took a deep breath. She tugged gently on the belt of her bathrobe and loosened the only shield she had.

"Oh my!" Delta gasped as she sloshed whiskey on the floor while pouring herself a second glass. "Now, please tell me this is not your wedding dress. It's a crime, Izzie, an absolutely atrocious crime, and I'm not letting you go out there looking like that."

"My mother made it for me," Isabel explained blandly, knowing there was no hope.

"Oh," Delta said, her bottom lip disappearing as she nibbled on it in panic. "I'm sorry. Your face is stunning enough for people not to look at your dress."

"Everyone looks at the dress! It's like the one thing they all focus on, photograph and talk about the entire day!" Isabel shrieked at her. She took a deep breath and steadied herself. "Sorry, I'm just a little wound up."

"It's not that bad," Delta assured her. "The peach bows cover most of the really bad parts."

Isabel's mother had come up with the genius solution of stitching the shreds of fabric back together with some peach ribbon that she just had several hundred rolls of.

"Are you sure you want to wear the furry jacket, though?" Delta asked with a frown. "It's sweltering outside, and you might faint… again. You really can't afford any more bruising." Her eyes darted to Isabel's purple forehead.

Isabel glared at her and pulled open the faux fur white overlay, revealing her hooker Bo-peep corset set-up. Delta's gasp was enough for Isabel to whip the jacket closed again.

"Now you understand," Isabel snapped, allowing herself another miniscule sip of her whiskey.

"I think Ricardo would totally understand if you arrived drunk for your own wedding, all things considered," Delta teased.

Isabel was famous for her ridiculously low tolerance for alcohol, which was why she was so careful to only drink on very rare occasions, and in tiny amounts.

"No," Isabel shook her head, "I have to remember the real importance of this day. I get to marry the man of my dreams and spend forever with him."

"Well, at least you know you will get married. After the world sees me in this," she gestured to her meringue shaped dress, "I'm going to be declared a spinstress immediately."

Isabel felt the tension drain off her shoulders as she and Delta giggled over their dresses and the unfortunate disaster that had become her wedding day.

"I know many people think you're weak for letting your mother, and mother-in-law, walk all over you," Delta began.

"Hey!" Isabel complained with mock offense.

"But I think you're pretty impressive for focusing on what's really important, beyond all the pomp and showy display that the bridal industry makes billions off."

A bell sounded outside, signaling for guests to take their seats and wait for a supposedly spectacular bride. Isabel could hear her mother's voice outside frantically ordering people to 'get out of the way'.

"Thanks, Delta. Well, it seems like this is it," Isabel said with a wan smile. "I totally understand if you want to abandon me and hide safely away in here."

Delta thrust her shoulders back and struck a model pose.

"And miss the chance to stand next to my best friend on the day of her wedding?" she laughed. "I don't think so. We're in this together."

Isabel let out a wavering sigh of relief. She took another small sip of whiskey, her face pulling at the bitter taste, while Delta got in at least another two shots. Her maid of honor was leaning towards the tipsy side by the time Violet knocked on the door and summoned them.

Her mother-in-law to-be was ashen-faced and her top lip trembled as she spoke. Her mind was clearly elsewhere, and she had a vague, distracted look in her eyes.

"It's time, my dear," she said in a half whisper to Isabel.

"Are you alright?" Isabel asked. "You look like you've seen the dead?"

"In a way, I have," Violet muttered before forcing an unconvincing smile onto her dazed face. "We're going to be late, come along."

***

Isabel took a deep breath. The heat outside was stifling, and she could feel the sweat rolling between her shoulder blades and down her bare back. Her armpits were wet inside the faux fur jacket, and she wondered again if she should simply remove it and look like a hooker on her wedding day.

"Are you okay?" her father, Robert, asked, noticing his daughter had been fidgeting and scratching for at least five minutes.

"Sure," Isabel panted. "Why?"

"Your face is turning red, and you look like you're about to faint."

"I'm just a little hot," she admitted, wiping the film of sweat off her clammy forehead. She could feel the damp curls going limp around her face.

"Delta, you'd better get this show on the road before we lose our bride."

Isabel watched as Delta, who'd been instructed to walk with a goose, wearing a giant peach bow around its neck, approached the red carpeted aisle that floated atop the green lawn. Isabel bit her lip as Delta walked unsteadily through the guests, wafting whiskey at all of them as she smiled and waved confidently.

Everything was proceeding relatively smoothly until a drunken Delta stepped on the tail feathers of the goose. The goose retaliated instantly with a rather vicious peck at Delta's bare knee, causing her to squeal in fright and leap onto Pedro. Pedro was happy to wrap his arms around the slender damsel in distress, causing his date to glare at them with tangible envy.

The goose, dissatisfied with a single peck, located the airborne Delta, and began jumping up to continue its attack. Delta kicked wildly at the flapping, feathery fiend, causing one of her shoes to fling off and whack one guest on the head. The entire flock of geese charged into the ceremony, ready to attack, as if the other geese had sensed the tail feather incident.

Isabel watched in horror as the orderly rows of guests erupted into screaming chaos and people ran over each other to escape from flying shoes and snapping geese.

"Stop!" a powerful voice bellowed over the noise.

Every person froze, as though powerless to disobey the commanding voice of Colleen Austin. Even the offended geese seemed to obey, their tiny beady eyes homing in on Colleen. Violet quickly stepped in to secure the pieces of rope around their necks and led the geese safely away.

"Need I remind you we are assembled here today for my daughter's wedding. Please stop running around like headless chickens, turn your chairs back over, and resume your seat promptly!" Colleen commanded as though she had the authority of an army general.

Rachel, Ricardo's detective partner and best 'woman', was fighting hard not to roar with laughter at the entire ceremony. She whispered, what Isabel hoped were a few reassuring words into Ricardo's ear. The guests scurried in quiet obedience to rearrange their seats and sit down. Within seconds, everything was as it should be.

Delta, barefoot, since her shoes could not be located after the minor disturbance, recommenced her swaying walk down the aisle and arrived at the altar without further obstruction. Isabel watched as hundreds of pairs of eyes unexpectedly turned to watch her grand entrance next.

"You can do this," Robert, her father, whispered into her ear.

"I look ridiculous," Isabel mumbled back at him. She could feel her heart practically humming in her chest. It was beating so fast.

"Nonsense," he chided her gently. "My darling girl," he took her by the arms, "even the most stunning dress in the world would pale compared to your natural beauty. You look like the most beautiful woman in the world."

Isabel felt hot tears well up and she had to wick them away quickly with her father's handkerchief before they washed away any more of her make-up. She had already sweated most of it off.

"Anytime now, Rob," Isabel's mother hissed at them down the aisle. There was a ripple of polite laughter from the guests.

Robert tugged on Isabel's arm and the pair made their slow walk down the aisle, in time with the gentle pings of a harp. Isabel smiled dutifully at the 'ooh-ing' and 'ah-ing' guests, but she soon fixed her focus on the man at the end of her long walk: Ricardo Finch.

Ricardo beamed at her with absolute love, his mouth in a broad smile and his eyes rapidly blinking away tears. A loud cough broke her focus momentarily, but Isabel kept looking at Ricardo. She felt woozy from the intense sauna she was living inside, thanks to the jacket, and she worried that she really would faint before making it to the altar.

There was another cough, and then another, as though someone was choking. Isabel forced her smile to not to waver, and she picked up the pace. The harpist jumped up the speed of her playing to suit the hurried rhythm of Isabel's charge down the aisle. She could feel the guests around her fidget as the coughing grew louder and more frantic, drowning out the peaceful melody.

The coughing stopped.

It was replaced with a scream that pierced through the lazy, hot afternoon air. Isabel spun around, heaving heavy folds of fabric with her, so that she could scan the rows of guests. Her eyes flitted from one confused face to the next until she located the group of faces that displayed more alarm and panic. Finally, she settled her gaze on a pale Rosemary, who was quivering from head to toe. A trembling hand pointed at the ground.

Micky lay at her feet, crumpled in between the chairs.

Rosemary had two fingers on his wrist. Her face was white as she delivered the words, "He's dead!"

Chapter 4
Death by Cinnamon

The advantage of marrying an officer of the law was that Ricardo was trained to spring into action at any moment, even if that moment was his wedding ceremony. Ricardo gave the nod to Rachel, who immediately pulled out a mobile phone that was strapped to her thigh underneath her elegant gown. Within seconds, the police had been alerted, and an ambulance was on the way.

Rachel then cleared a space around the body so that Micky could easily be attended to. Ricardo, wedding jacket off and sleeves rolled up, was on his knees, trying to resuscitate Micky. Isabel stood by, anxiously watching as her future husband worked to save one of her guests. Her fur jacket became a comfortable cushion for Rosemary to sob into.

Even after the ambulance arrived and took over affairs, there was no hope of bringing Micky back to life. Isabel Austin, for she was still an Austin and not yet a Finch, watched as the paramedics declared one of her guests undeniably dead.

Most brides would have crumbled under the disappointment or thrown a tantrum that their special day had been ruined. The more fanatically determined brides would have had the body removed and forced the ceremony to continue, as though nothing less than spectacular had occurred on their precious day.

But not Isabel Austin.

Isabel had seen her fair share of dead bodies. After arriving in Cyprus Cove and having to solve a case that involved her own life, Isabel had tagged along, and usually solving several police murder cases. She still had the cold, hard memory of tripping over the very first dead body she had ever encountered. In her experience of finding dead bodies, they had always come to mean murder. It was therefore not unusual that Isabel's inquisitive brain was drawn to investigate whether Micky had died of natural causes, or possibly something more sinister.

"Isabel," Colleen said, stopping Isabel's approach to the body. "We need to calm your guests down and get this show on the road."

"A man just died," Isabel replied in shock. "We can't just continue with the wedding as though nothing has happened."

Her mother blinked at her a few times, as though Isabel's words could not register in Colleen's brain.

"But why not? People drop dead all the time. I simply don't see why we should let that alter our plans."

"What if he didn't simply 'drop dead'," Isabel snapped. "I need to see the body."

"Isabel Eliza May Austin, you will do no such thing!" her mother commanded.

Isabel always knew the severity of her mother's instruction by how many of her names she had employed.

"I'm sorry, but I need to know. I'm not a little girl anymore, Mom. You need to let me do what I need to do," Isabel informed her mother as directly as she could before ducking under the barrier tape Rachel had set up, her eyes fixed on the prostrate body stretched across the lawn.

She could vaguely hear her mother spitting angry words at her from the other side of the tape, but a single glance at the dead body set Colleen off, threatening to faint, and so Isabel was left in silence.

"You shouldn't be here," Ricardo said as soon as he spotted her. "This is your wedding day!"

"The last time I checked, it was yours too," she said with a small smile, despite the gravity of the situation. "God wouldn't allow us to get married unless we solved one last case together as single people."

Ricardo smiled. "You look radiantly beautiful."

"You're lying," Isabel accused. "Do you think he died of natural causes?

"You tell me. What do you deduce about the body?"

Isabel took a step closer, her eyes absorbing as many details of the scene as she could. She tried to assemble these facts to mean something. "His skin is all red and swollen around his mouth."

"Apparently too many cherry pies."

"No," Isabel shook her head. "His skin isn't stained. It's a rash. Like he was allergic to something. Look at how swollen his neck is, too. He couldn't breathe anymore."

"Perhaps he choked."

"I don't think so," Isabel disagreed. "I think he had an allergic reaction to something he ate."

"The paramedics concluded the same."

"Rosemary," Isabel called her over from the paramedics, who were treating her for shock. "Did Micky have any allergies that you knew about?"

Rosemary thought for a while, her face scrunched up as she forced her shocked mind to concentrate.

"I know that there was something I could never cook with. I just can't think what," Rosemary replied.

"We can try to access his medical records," Rachel suggested.

"Or we could check his wallet," Isabel guessed. "People with life-threatening allergies usually have a bracelet or a tag in their wallet."

Ricardo whipped a medical glove on and stooped down next to Micky. He poked two fingers through each blazer pocket and pulled out a worn leather wallet. This he carefully opened and flipped through.

"Ricardo," Isabel called him after the minutes ticked by.

It was as though he had frozen. His eyes stared forward, unblinking, and his posture remained hunched over the wallet, as though he could not believe what he was seeing.

"What's going on?" Isabel asked again after receiving no response.

"Earth to detective Finch," Rachel teased him. "Wake up, man!"

Isabel noticed a slight shake in the hand that held the wallet, and she instantly knew that something was very wrong. She lifted the front of her dress, bows and all, and inched closer to him.

"Ricardo, honey, do you have to spring into investigation mode, even on your wedding day?" Violet said, scolding her son from the edge of the tape. "Let the paramedics handle it."

Ricardo's stare flitted briefly to her and then back to the body lying at his feet. Violet noticed his strange behavior and followed his gaze to Micky. She paled and hid her face behind her hands.

"What's troubling you?" Isabel whispered next to him.

Ricardo tilted his hand so that Isabel could see what he was fixated on. There was a small square photograph in Micky's wallet. It was of a little boy with bleached blonde hair, wide, happy, green eyes, and a wide smile. He looked as though he spent every day on the beach, surfing the waves and collecting shells.

Isabel tore her eyes from the photograph and looked at her fiancé. His blonde hair had darkened a little with age and working indoors, but the green eyes and smile she knew so well were unmistakable.

"Why does Micky have a photograph of you in his wallet?" Isabel stumbled over the awkward question.

"I don't know," Ricardo managed in between long pauses.

"There's a medical tag too," Isabel pointed out, hoping to distract everyone from Ricardo's odd behavior.

Her fingers deftly removed the wallet from Ricardo's shaking fingers, and she swiped out the tag and read, "He's allergic to cinnamon."

There was an audible gasp from the ring of people surrounding the body. Isabel thought it bizarre that an inoffensive spice like cinnamon could actually kill a person, but then again, she had seen people die from far stranger methods.

"Yes," Rosemary snapped her fingers, "that's why he was always so careful with which desserts he ate. Was there cinnamon in the food?"

Isabel chewed on her lip while she tried to force her scrambled brain to think. She felt as though she was overheating from the inside out and sweat dripped from her hairline and her cheeks felt on fire.

"I can't say if any of the food contained cinnamon because the catering was out of my hands," Isabel explained almost tearfully.

"There was no cinnamon," Colleen reported confidently. "Apparently Violet doesn't like it."

"That's true," Ricardo confirmed vaguely. "My mother is not a fan of cinnamon, so it's likely she would've requested it not be used in any of the food."

"Right, well, accidents happen. So, we should probably talk to the caterer," she said in between slight wheezes.

"Are you alright, dear?" her mother asked her.

"Just peachy," Isabel replied, cringing at the accidental reference to the most popular color at her wedding.

"There's an officer locating the caterers right now," Rachel informed them. "And they settled all the guests in Delta's lounge, sipping tea."

The fiery detective hauled out a notebook from another secret crevice of her dress, and she began taking copious notes of everything she could see around the body.

"Rosemary," Isabel addressed her, "did you see what Micky ate at the snacks table?"

Rosemary's lips trembled, and she shut her eyes tightly while she tried to think. "I only saw him eat the cherry pies. Most of the options were savory, anyway, and everyone knows Micky has a sweet tooth."

"Did you taste a cherry pie?"

Rosemary nodded. "I did."

"Do you recall tasting cinnamon?"

Rosemary covered her face with her hands while she replayed the joyful events from less than an hour before, when her close romantic friend was still alive and dusting pastry crumbs off his blazer.

"I'm sorry, Izzie, I just don't know. It's just too much to take in right now."

"There, there, dear," Colleen soothed, swooping into rescuing Rosemary from her distress. "Let's go inside and I'll make you a cup of tea to settle your nerves. I'm sure we can find a shot of something stronger to help calm you down."

Isabel nodded gratefully as her mother ushered Rosemary into the cool interior of Delta's tearoom.

"You're not looking so great yourself," Rachel pointed out to Isabel.

"I'm fine, really," Isabel claimed while dragging the corner of her jacket across her forehead to soak up the sweat.

"Why not take off your jacket?" Rachel urged her.

"I'm fine!" Isabel snapped. "Look, the caterer is here."

"I'm head chef Francisco," he introduced himself. "I've mainly dealt with the mothers of the bride and groom."

"I suppose I need to humbly apologize then," Isabel joked faintly, and soon had to cringe away from Violet's hurt glare.

"Uhm, the cherry pies. Did your staff add any cinnamon to them, chef?"

"No," he replied confidently.

"I'm sorry," Rachel said without the slightest hint of remorse in her voice, "but how can you be sure someone didn't slip a little cinnamon into one of the snacks served?"

"I spoke to my kitchen staff, and no one used cinnamon. Then the officer searched the kitchen himself and no cinnamon was found. None of our recipes contained it, so why would we need to add it?"

"What about the cherry pies?" Rachel charged.

"No cinnamon."

"You're positive?"

"Absolutely," Francisco replied, his muscular arms folding across his chest.

Rachel would not accept defeat. She stalked through the garden, her heels puncturing holes into the grass as she walked, until she reached the welcoming table, where she grabbed a plate of leftover cherry pies. With a smirk across her face, she marched back to the caterer and offered him the plate.

"Yes, detective?" Francisco asked politely, a crease forming on his brow.

"Can you detect any cinnamon?" she demanded, as if holding the plate under his nose made that obvious.

Isabel was trying to get closer to Ricardo, who had remained pallid and mute for much of the conversation. She noticed he kept staring at the childhood photograph of himself. Her legs did not want to move under the heavy fabric they draped her in, and she was feeling claustrophobic inside the stifling jacket.

Rachel was loudly ordering the poor caterer to taste a pie, and after he hesitated a moment too long, Rachel seized the opportunity to shove one of the pies into his mouth.

The caterer glowered at her before his eyes widened with realization, followed by panic. He pulled the pie out of his mouth and examined the glossy cherries closely. He gasped with fright, and then declared a single word to the group, which confirmed their worst fears.

"Cinnamon!"

"Inside or on the surface?" Isabel asked quickly.

"On the surface!" he answered, his dark eyes studying the light brown cinnamon flecks that were just visible.

Rachel punched the air while Isabel shared a knowing look with Ricardo.

"Thank you for your help," Isabel informed the caterer. "Please return to the kitchen."

"Would you like us to continue preparing the starter and main course?" he asked uncertainly.

Isabel hesitated for a second, her eye catching Ricardo's. She smiled sadly, knowing the wedding was officially off, and turned back to the caterer. "I think our guests are hungry and they're going to be here for some time while the detectives question them. It might be best to keep them happy with some good food. We will continue the menu as planned."

"Yes, ma'am," came the non-judgmental reply, before the caterer hurried back to his post.

"Are you thinking what I'm thinking?" Isabel asked Ricardo and Rachel as they huddled around her. She could feel her already hot body temperature soar even higher.

"That your dress is seriously ugly?" Rachel pointed out bluntly.

"Rachel!" Ricardo scolded her, though even he struggled to hide the distaste from his own expression.

"I'm not offended," Isabel replied mildly in between pants. Rachel's right. But I was actually talking more along the lines of the cause of Micky's demise."

"There was no cinnamon in the kitchen," Ricardo repeated the fact.

"There was no cinnamon in the pies," Rachel added.

"And yet there was," Isabel pointed out, her hand wiping the sweat from her forehead. "*Someone* added it intentionally, knowing it would be harmless to all other guests except one, with a sweet tooth. And we all know what that means."

"Boycott cinnamon?" Rachel joked.

"No, we have a murderer in our midst!" Isabel declared with a breathless mixture of both fear and excitement.

Chapter 5
The Hunt for a Killer

After the starters were served and nervously devoured by starved guests, the police rounded them up and announced that the wedding was officially postponed, because of circumstances well beyond that of the bride and groom.

"Micky Robson, a guest here tonight, and friend of many," Ricardo was saying in a tone numb of emotion, "apparently died from an allergic reaction to cinnamon."

There was an expected gasp of horror that rang round the assembled group, the kind of response every bride dreams of hearing on her wedding day.

"The caterer and head chef both confirm that there was not supposed to be cinnamon in any of the dishes served this afternoon, yet someone," Ricardo paused and looked intently from face to face, "dusted the cherry pies in cinnamon powder."

Another predictable gasp rippled through the guests as they turned on each other with accusatory glances.

"The death of Micky Robson was no accident, and it has therefore been declared a murder case, and will be investigated as such, unless further evidence suggests otherwise," Ricardo announced with finality.

The audience offered a stunned look in response, many of them gaping openly at their honorable groom who had transformed into an intimidating detective who could, at any moment, accuse them of murder and drag them off to the jailhouse.

"Basically," Rachel interrupted in her candid fashion, "every one of you is a suspect and will be interrogated by the police. There's no point refusing to cooperate, because no one gets to leave until we have found the killer. So, the faster one of you fesses up, the faster we can get on with our lives and go home."

This did not go down well, and there was an immediate uproar. Angry fists shook in the air, hysterical women sobbed, and there was even a scream or two of fright.

"That was tactful," Isabel muttered to Rachel.

Isabel was still constricted by her frightful wedding dress and the sweaty faux fur jacket. Her forehead was clammy, and she was feeling dizzy after the many gallons of water she had sweated out of her system.

"What did I say?" Rachel demanded gruffly. "People are so sensitive these days."

"Please," Isabel spoke up, "make yourselves comfortable in our host's beautiful home, but do not wander beyond the boundary the police have set out for you. You have access to food and drink, as well as ablution facilities. If you have questions, please talk to me -"

"I have a question," Debbie interrupted loudly and with a swish of her see-through leopard dress. "When can I leave? I have other far more exciting places to be, especially since this one turned out to be such a drab bore."

There were a few chuckles at Debbie's rude response, but mostly the guests glared at her.

"Well, since you weren't invited to this event in the first place," Isabel snapped, feeling her cheeks catch fire from the suffocating dress and from the embarrassment Debbie had thrust her way, "you have little room to make demands, Deborah."

"Since I'm technically not an invited guest, surely that means I'm not the killer," Debbie chuckled in her raspy smoker's voice, "so I can slip out the way I slipped in?"

The heavily made-up Debbie looked around for gathering supporters as she cackled away at her own joke.

"That's enough," a weepy Rosemary interrupted. "You may have brought yourself here of your own free will, but now you will respect the orders from the bride and groom!"

"As well as the detective running this case," Ricardo added with a dark scowl. "Perhaps we will begin our interviews with you, Deborah Bertha Smith," he said, reading her full name from a list.

Debbie's fickle followers quickly switched to the other side, offering their supportive chuckles to the detective. The old woman pursed her creased lips and stormed off to the bar.

While Ricardo was organizing the proceedings for progressive interviews to begin, Isabel slipped away to do some investigating of her own. She soon found what she was looking for: a heap of bags belonging to guests and left unattended in the sunroom. Among these were many colorful gift bags and presents that the guests had brought along to hand over to the newlywed couple.

Isabel shot a cautious look around the vacant room before flicking her fingers through the various paper packages.

"Gorgeous!" Isabel gasped, as she drew out a sculpture of three cats.

She did not have to look at the tag to know Thomas, her close friend and companion in the art world, had hand sculptured her three beloved feline pets as a wedding gift for her and Ricardo. A surge of guilt washed over her as she realized she was searching through gifts her guests had brought her hoping to find evidence to pinpoint one of them as a killer.

Her keen desire to find the killer and uncover the injustice that had taken place far surpassed her respect for her friends and guests. Besides, there was the odd connection between Ricardo and Micky, which she also needed to figure out quickly. As Isabel worked her way silently through the gifts, her mind weaved through the assortment of interactions she had witnessed during the wedding.

She thought of the pallor of Violet's skin after her brash encounter with Micky at the snacks table. Suspicions crept into her mind. Dangerous suspicions. She felt a shiver rake her skin despite the damp fur jacket that clung to her skin and made her come out in hives.

Isabel continued her search through the bags and boxes until her nose drew her to a clue more than her fingers.

"Cinnamon!" she hissed to herself.

She rummaged more fanatically until she stopped at a gift bag that filled the air with the spicy aroma of cinnamon.

Isabel pulled out the bottle of brown ground cinnamon with glee, holding it up as though she had won an Oscar for best performance. Her eyes sprinted round for the identifying tag and, upon spotting the name, Isabel's stomach dropped to her knees, and she felt as though she would be sick.

This was the final straw for the over-excited bride who had endured too much on her wedding day. The savage heat that had berated her without letup led to a scarlet-colored and sweaty Isabel crumpling to the floor, with heaps of heavy and hideous fabric pooling around her. With shaky fingers, a panting Isabel wrenched open the buttons of the soaked fur jacket and threw the smelly, wet pile of sodden fur away from her. Isabel relished the rush of cool air that blew against her blistered skin. She scratched at the tight corset constricting her breathing and could stand it no longer. Her fingers tore at the fabric until she had ripped the uncomfortable bodice clean off herself.

"I can breathe!" Isabel gasped in euphoric celebration, as she felt her aching ribs expand to full capacity for the first time since they had stuffed her into the dress.

Isabel kicked off the heavy fabric and felt a hundred times lighter, skipping round the room in her silk petticoat.

"What are you doing?" Ricardo asked, stepping into the sunroom, and flanked by a couple of officers that respectfully averted their gaze from their boss's half-naked wife-to-be.

"I was…" Isabel stammered, her overheated brain backtracking to the moment that had set off her desperate need to escape her imprisoning dress. "I found a bottle of cinnamon shoved into one of the gift bags. The seal was broken, and it had definitely been used."

"To whom did the bag belong?"

Isabel swallowed. This was the part she had been dreading.

"Pedro," she half-whispered, knowing how much the answer would hurt Ricardo. "It was in his bag."

Ricardo paled drastically, but he turned stiffly and gave the officer next to him the nod to summon Pedro to the first interview.

"It can't be him," Isabel said in a low voice. "Pedro has been one of your closest friends for years. What motive would he have for killing a complete stranger, and with cinnamon? How would he have known to use such a bizarre murder weapon?"

"We have to follow the clues," Ricardo reasoned quietly, his voice eerily devoid of emotion.

Isabel knew there was no point in reasoning with him. She nodded calmly and said, "You speak to Pedro, and I'll see what else I can find."

"Iz?" Ricardo called her back to him.

"Yeah?"

"As much as I enjoy your current outfit, it might be best if you find something more suitable to wear."

Isabel looked down, having completely forgotten she was wearing only a slip.

***

Isabel had traversed the depths of Delta's enormous walk-in closet, to find something plain and inexpensive. She realized that her entire apartment could fit into Delta's closet, with room to spare.

Once decently clothed, Isabel wound her way through the floors of Delta's intricate home until she found a safe spot to spy on the guests. A high-pitched scream from the sunroom interrupted her thoughts.

Fearing another murder and with her heart pounding in her chest, Isabel sprinted after the scream, her eyes scanning the room and refusing to blink until she had found out that no one else was dead.

Her mother lay crumpled on the floor, her face hidden, and her wails muffled by folds of peach-colored fabric. Isabel ran to her, thinking her mother hurt. She dropped to her knees at her mother's side.

"What's wrong?" Isabel asked, her hands gently pulling her mother's face towards her.

"My dress!" she screamed again. "I spent hours stitching it for you, and it's all ripped up by a savage beast. I ask you, what kind of murderer would do something like this?"

As Isabel contemplated her mother's mascara-stained cheeks, her clumped up false eyelashes, and her smudged and trembling bottom lip, she decided that the truth could wait.

"I don't know," Isabel uttered the lie. "I took it off so that it wouldn't get damaged during the investigation. I can't think who would have done this…" Isabel trailed off unconvincingly, the lie twisting her insides.

Isabel Austin, while professing to be a model citizen with good moral standards, had lied occasionally to investigate a case. But she had never been in the habit of lying to her own mother, largely out of fearful respect for what her mother would do to her when she inevitably found out the truth.

"I will inform Ricardo immediately. He must uncover whoever did this to my dress. Oh, Izzy," her mother sobbed again, with a wave of fresh tears flowing down her plump cheeks, "what will you wear to your wedding?"

"Let's not worry about that now," she assured her mother. "Why don't you settle down with a nice cup of tea and leave the investigating to Ricardo and I."

"Of course, dear," her mother nodded tearfully. "You're the best daughter I've ever had."

"I'm your *only* daughter," Isabel muttered as she nuzzled her mother out of the sunroom.

"Oh, there's one more thing I wanted to tell you," Colleen remembered suddenly. "I came here to give you some information about the case."

"Okay," Isabel replied doubtfully. She knew her mother was a raging gossiper, and therefore scrutinized other people so that she could absorb information on them to use during her gossip sessions. Isabel would not discount the information her mother uncovered, though she would take it with a pinch of salt.

"I saw your little gray friend, Rosey," her mother said in a low voice, "arguing with that Micky shortly before the ceremony started."

"My Rosemary?"

"Yes, "Colleen confirmed. "I thought it was odd because Micky was her date and then shortly after fighting, he drops dead."

"But he would've eaten the cinnamon coated cherry pies long before that," Isabel pointed out.

"An allergy which Rosemary admitted knowing," Colleen continued with a raised eyebrow, emphasizing her suspicions.

"Rosey said she knew he had an allergy, but that she couldn't remember what -"

"That's exactly what I'd say if *I* was the killer," Colleen countered with a prim smile. "I'm just saying Ricardo is apparently questioning one of his close friends. It's only fair that you set side your bias and do the same."

Isabel scowled at her mother and grit her teeth, but when the folds of destroyed wedding dress fabric caught her eye, she lowered her gaze and nodded mutely.

"I'll chat with her."

***

Her talk with Rosemary was more of an emotional fit, rather than a casual chat.

"Just because I had an argument with him, doesn't mean I tried to kill him!" Rosemary argued heatedly.

"Of course not," Isabel said, trying to quiet Rosemary down, "but I need to know what you were discussing with Micky, and why it upset you so much."

Rosemary released a vicious sigh and folded her arms stubbornly. Isabel shifted her hand to Rosemary's forearm and smiled at her emotionally wrought friend.

"I was arguing with him about his long list of women from the past," Rosemary explained sadly.

"He's an older guy, so it makes sense that he would've had quite a few relationships prior to you," Isabel considered calmly.

"No," Rosemary shook her head, "it was more than that. Violet," she almost spat the name, "nearly erupted when she encountered Micky among the guests. She looked as though she had bumped into a ghost. I confronted her about her reaction, and the woman was borderline mental! She told me I should watch myself, because Micky had had his fair share of women and none of them ended well."

"I know that must have been difficult to hear from another woman, but Violet doesn't make things up. She's as honest as they come. What did you do next?" Isabel asked carefully.

Rosemary fixed Isabel with a long, hard stare. "I didn't kill him, if that's what you're implying!" Rosemary snapped, her voice quavering dangerously with heavy emotion.

Isabel slipped a comforting arm around her old friend's shoulders and tried to steady her.

"I'm not. I do not know who killed him. Ricardo is following a lead regarding the cinnamon, and I'm trying to understand who Micky really was, and why someone killed him for that."

Rosemary let out a long sigh. "I asked Micky about Violet's accusation. And do you know what he did? He laughed at me and shrugged it off!"

"Oh dear," Isabel groaned, knowing exactly what Micky had meant by that.

"He claimed that a 'dashing fellow' like himself couldn't be expected to remain tied down to one woman. He admitted he had been with plenty of women in the past and, to make matters worse, he looked proud of it!" Rosemary exploded with indignation, which was swiftly followed by a wave of sadness.

"I'm so sorry," Isabel apologized. "At least this makes it somewhat easier to let go of him, now that he's… you know…"

Rosemary provided her with an incensed snort. "I wasn't finished. Micky and I argued before he died, but we also made-up." Her features softened to the old Rosemary, who had very much been in love with Micky. "Micky said that he no longer had the desire to chase after other women, because he was the happiest with me. That's why he returned early from his sail around the world. He wanted to be there for me at the wedding."

Isabel felt a lump well up in her throat. Rosemary's touching story was even more tragic since Micky had died, rendering their newly discovered love forever incomplete.

"Unfortunately, the past sometimes catches up with a person, even after a person feels they've changed," Isabel said in what she hoped was a tone of consolation.

"Micky didn't deserve to die!" Rosemary responded tartly.

"I'm sorry, Rose. I didn't mean it like that!"

Rosemary's beautiful face crumpled into a million fragile lines as she wept over the loss of something that could have been but was snatched away too quickly.

Isabel left Rosemary to mourn, while she targeted the next person she needed to talk to. She had decided that her suspicion about Micky would only grow more dangerous the longer it remained locked up in her questioning mind. She needed to resolve her gnawing concerns, and there were only two people in the world who could do that.

One of which was now dead.

"I need to talk to you," Isabel said in a low voice as she approached Ricardo's mother from behind.

Violet jolted in fright, the generous serving of port spilling all over her fingers.

"Izzie, you scared me half to death," she chuckled, without humor. "I was just having a little something to calm my nerves after all this murder business."

Isabel knew that Violet rarely indulged in alcohol unless it was a special occasion. To see her guzzling away at her port as though it was nothing more than iced tea was quite jarring.

"Are you okay?" Isabel began gently, her eyes watching the level of port.

"Apart from a dead body destroying my son's wedding day, I'm just fine," she cooed in an uncomfortably strangled voice.

"Ricardo is shaken up too," Isabel offered, hoping Violet would appreciate not being alone in her feelings.

"I don't see why," Violet responded stiffly. "He is a homicide detective, so he's fairly used to dealing with dead bodies."

"I think it's more to do with finding an old photograph of himself as a young boy in the victim's wallet," Isabel pointed out candidly, her eyes observing Violet's reaction to her words.

Violet splashed more port on the floor, her face paling at the reminder. She reached for the bottle on the bar and refilled her glass with a shaking hand.

"Ricardo does not know who his father is," Isabel continued, her eyes never leaving Violet's face. "But *you* do."

"Ricardo's father died in the army. He was an honorable soldier who fought bravely -"

"You underestimate your son's skills as a detective. He investigated the story you fed him as a child, years ago, and discovered it was entirely fictional."

Isabel bit her tongue. She knew she had already gone too far and was meddling between her future husband and his mother, but if they were going to become family, then the truth needed to be uncovered, no matter how difficult it was to cough up and deal with.

Violet took a long swig of her port and looked as though she was going to faint, either from intoxication or from Isabel's sensitive questions.

"The photograph of Ricardo in Micky's wallet. Why was it there?"

"I don't know why you keep bringing that up…" Violet replied unconvincingly.

"I think you do. I think that's why you got into a fight with Rosemary. You tried to warn her to stay away from Micky because he worked his way through all women. You knew that to be true, because you were one woman he left behind," Isabel pressed further.

Violet dissolved into tears, her near empty glass of port dropping to the grass. "What will my son think of me?" she cried, her body shuddering with unleashed emotion that had been pent up for years.

"I think your son would admire you all the more for telling him the truth about his father. He's been searching for him his whole life. You can finally give him peace of mind."

"How will it give him 'peace of mind' knowing he came from a man like Micky? A man who thrived on seeing how many women he could woo, impregnate, and then thrust aside as though it were all meaningless. Ricardo would be so ashamed to know where he came from."

"I doubt that. Your son has a lot of you in him. You're the one who raised him and impacted who he is today. Micky has no claim on any of that. You shaped Ricardo. *You* were and still are the parent who has never left his side. Micky is simply his biological father."

Violet shivered after hearing her darkest secret stated out loud as an open fact for everyone to snigger and whisper about behind her back. She fired a furtive look over her shoulder, as though the bushes were concealing a reporter ready to publish her news for the world to document and pass judgement on.

"Would you keep your voice down!" Violet snapped at her.

"You need to tell Ricardo."

"He doesn't need to know. Micky is dead anyway, so what's the point," Violet insisted.

"Well, as his future wife, I don't feel I can keep this information from him. So, either you tell him, or I will." Isabel felt her heart pound against her chest with every word she forced out. It was not in her nature to stand up to people, especially those of the mother or mother-in-law type. Sweat broke out on her forehead and she tried to hide the tremor in her hand.

Violet shook her head and laughed. "No, you won't. You're smart, but you're kind and timid. I know you've grown up a lot since you've been following Ricardo around on his murder cases, but you won't go against my wishes and tell him a truth that's not yours to tell. It's just not in your nature."

Isabel clenched her jaw tightly. She could feel her fists ball up, and she wanted to deny every word Violet had said. Isabel was certain she had grown on her own, in the last year, and not simply because she had been in a relationship with Ricardo, but because she had found her own strength.

"Is that a chance you're willing to take?" Isabel asked in a wavering voice. "I mean, do you really think my love for Ricardo is so easily conquered by my own inner fears and failings? Of course, I'm timid and abiding. I allowed you and Mom to do whatever you wanted with *my* wedding, because the dress and décor were far more important to the pair of you than they ever were to me. But with Ricardo, it will not force me to hide the truth from him. He deserves to know, and as his wife, I plan to make sure he does."

"You're not his wife yet," Violet cautioned her, with a severe look that hurled all her inner strength at Isabel's defenses.

Isabel decided against responding to the idle threat that had been pointedly cast her way. Violet was clearly emotional after being blatantly confronted by her past, especially on a day which focused on the future. She chose instead to pull a tense Violet into a forced hug.

"I cannot even imagine how hard life has been for you, especially having a man walk out on you while you were with child."

Violet relaxed slightly in her arms, holding Isabel for a moment before withdrawing again. Violet's face was wet with tears. Isabel's gentleness in the face of an attack had broken her.

"Micky and I were happy for a time," she admitted in a low voice. "He asked me to marry him, and I agreed. I loved him very much. He was so full of life and charm. He promised me forever together." Her eyes filled with tears again.

Isabel was shocked at the how quickly Violet's hostility had evaporated. "Then what went wrong?"

"Another woman claimed that Micky was the father of her child. She demanded he wed her immediately before the child was born. The girl's family got involved, and it was a mess, so to save my reputation, I quietly stepped out."

"Wait," Isabel interrupted, confusion furrowing her brow. "Did Micky know about Ricardo?"

Violet shook her head sadly. "I didn't know about Ricardo myself until he was already married to the other woman. I didn't have the heart to tell him after that. So I kept my pregnancy a secret."

"How awful for you!" Isabel cried, feeling her own heart break. "But Micky had the photograph, so how did he find out?"

"I bumped into Micky when Ricardo was about six. Micky took one look at him and knew Ricardo was his. I wrote to

Micky and explained what happened. I sent him the photograph you saw in his wallet. I couldn't let him into Ricardo's life. Micky was divorced and running rogue by that stage. He wouldn't have been the role model Ricardo needed."

"How many of the women you know at this wedding have been in a relationship with Micky?"

Violet shook her head in disgust. "All the women round my age, and quite a few older. Minus your mother, of course, and any of the family and friends from out of town."

"That is quite a large pool of suspects to draw from," Isabel muttered.

"Do you think one of them killed Micky?"

"I do. It had to be someone he had been close to because they knew about the cinnamon allergy. Micky broke a lot of hearts," Isabel explained, "and that results in a lot of enemies."

"Are you implying that I'm a suspect too?"

Isabel swallowed her immediate response and replied, "Right now, everyone is a suspect."

Chapter 6
Confronting the Past

"Ricardo blew out of here in a foul mood," Rachel explained. "So did Pedro. I think the pair of them had a fight."

Rachel had hoisted up her elegant gown, so that they did not trap her rather shapely legs under the folds of fabric that would only slow her down. She was still wearing her dangerous heels and had a gun strapped to her upper thigh. Isabel thought she saw a pair of handcuffs strapped to the other thigh. Rachel, as always, was one of the most intimidating and highly respected detectives Isabel had ever encountered.

"Not surprising. It must be hard questioning a close friend when they're your first murder suspect," Isabel replied, forcing her mind back to the conversation.

"I guess. Men are complicated," Rachel stated with an impatient wave of her hand.

"Did you get some background info on Micky?"

Rachel grinned. "I did. Old Micky was a real wild guy in his day. Seems like he only really started settling down after meeting your old friend, Rosey."

"I'd gathered as much. Any obvious enemies?"

"Plenty. The guy was loaded with cash. Wouldn't say so to look at him, but that much money must have tempted someone to off him. Then there were the several women who maintained he was the father of their children, but Micky denied most claims."

"So, we should look for an angry ex or, even worse, some angry Micky spawn who may have wanted to avenge their abandoned mothers," Isabel reasoned, before suddenly realizing what the words escaping her mouth meant. She froze, her big brown eyes burning into Rachel's. "Did Ricardo see the file on Micky?"

"Yeah, he read the lot. Why?"

"Where is he now?" Isabel demanded.

"Delta refused to have a dead body in the freezer, so he's been transported to the morgue already."

Isabel stared blankly at Rachel. "Not Micky! Where is Ricardo?

Rachel snorted. "Oh, him. I have no idea, and I don't have time to keep track of your husband either."

"I need to find him," Isabel explained before dashing away from Rachel.

"How are you two ever going to get married if you both keep running away?" Rachel shouted after her.

Isabel ignored her. She was certain Ricardo's foul mood had not been due to interviewing Pedro, but because he had confirmed, based on evidence in Micky's file, that Micky was his biological father. There was only one place her husband-to-be would go to try to deal with something that enormous.

As warm beach sand slid between her toes, Isabel spotted a lone figure in the distance sitting on the shore.

"I thought I might find you here," Isabel said softly as she approached Ricardo.

He smiled briefly up at her before returning his intense stare to the endless waves that lapped just out of reach of his feet. He was still wearing his wedding suit pants, though he also wore his weapon and badge on his hip. Isabel wondered if he had packed them in his honeymoon bag, just in case. His shirt sleeves were rolled up, and he had lost his peach wedding tie.

"I needed some space to think," Ricardo muttered, his eyes avoiding hers.

"About?"

Ricardo brooded in silence.

"Let me guess," Isabel said gently, as she sat down next to him and slipped her hand into his, "the photograph in Micky's wallet."

Ricardo sighed loudly and she could feel his entire frame tense up next to her.

"It was easy to figure out after that," he said stiffly. "Micky and my mother…"

Words failed him and he shook his head.

"It's a lot to deal with in one day," Isabel soothed. "Not only finding out he's your father but having to solve his murder too."

Ricardo bowed his head between his knees to hide his tears. "I should've known you'd already figured it out long before me. How did you do it?"

"I forced a confession out of your mother," Isabel replied guiltily. "She will try to explain things later. Be kind. She's had a hard day too, and it's a lot to answer up to."

"I just can't believe I had a father all this time that I could've gotten to know," Ricardo said hoarsely. "And now, what's the point of even knowing when he's gone?"

"This case may help you learn what kind of man he was," Isabel attempted to cheer him up.

"Yeah, the kind that gets himself murdered because he's upset so many people in his lifetime," Ricardo replied with a surly shake of his head. "I wonder how many half-siblings I have out in the world."

"Regardless, Micky didn't deserve death. As his son, you can acknowledge and honor him by solving his murder."

This thought seemed to appeal to Ricardo, and his shoulders straightened and he sat upright.

"You're right. I should focus less on me, and more on trying to find whoever did this to the man who is technically my father."

Isabel smiled, relieved to see the softness returning to Ricardo's face.

"I love you," he whispered to her, his lips finding hers in the glowing warmth of the dying afternoon light.

"What was that for?" she giggled.

"For helping me through one of my darkest moments. I know that with us working together as a team, we can solve anything," he said earnestly, his eyes never leaving hers.

"A team," she smiled. "Even though we are split up most of the time, we still end up solving our cases together."

Ricardo sighed again. "What's one more case before our wedding?"

"Exactly," Isabel smiled warmly. "Any leads with Pedro?"

Ricardo's face darkened. "Let's just say the interview didn't go down too well. He had no clue who Micky was or why anyone would want to kill him."

"What about the cinnamon found in his gift bag?"

"He claimed he got me a bottle of expensive whiskey, so the cinnamon must have been slipped in by someone else."

"I suppose if he really was the killer and tried to slip cinnamon into the wedding, he would've just made it part of your gift, like a spice rack or something."

"Exactly, so until we figure out who put the cinnamon into his bag, it's a dead end."

"Any prints?"

"A million," Ricardo sighed again. "It was a common shop-bought brand, so a lot of hands passed over it. Nothing clear enough to lift."

"Look, I know this is a sensitive question, especially now, but you read Micky's file. Did any names pop up which matched our guest list? Or some of our uninvited guests, perhaps?"

Ricardo wiped a hand down his face, his eyes somber. "There were a few unfamiliar names of women who tried to get Micky to pay support for their illegitimate kids, but they couldn't produce any proof. And none of them are at our wedding."

"I'm going to begin by interviewing some of the female guests in Micky's target age group. It's quite a large bracket to work through, but someone has to be connected."

"Great," Ricardo approved. "They may feel more comfortable talking to a woman. Don't forget to include the staff working here today. Someone may have used our wedding as an opportunity to get closer to… the victim."

Isabel could tell Ricardo was still struggling to comprehend everything they had blasted him with in the last couple of hours. He had been expecting to toast his brand-new wife and offer an eloquent speech to all his guests. The most terrifying part of his evening was supposed to be the first dance, and yet here he was trying to understand how his unknown father had not only rocked up at his wedding but also dropped dead.

"Do you need some time?" Isabel asked gently, noting the endless creases that stretched across Ricardo's pensive brow.

"Please," he breathed in relief. "I just need to rearrange my thoughts before I try to approach this case with an objective mindset."

Isabel delivered a dutiful kiss and strode away slowly through the sand. Everyone had advised her that marriage was complex, but until that morning, she could not fathom why. Now she could see that it was not simply a matter of two people loving each other, but so many unforeseen factors could easily threaten the bond she had worked so hard to create.

Isabel silently resolved in her heart never to allow anything to ruin her marriage before it had even begun.

As she made her way up through the garden, she noticed most of the décor was in ruins. Her mother was chasing a rebellious goose around, which had already shredded most of the pretentious flower arrangements. Isabel decided she did not dislike geese as much as she initially thought. The ice sculpture had melted, and someone had trodden the peach ribbons in the dirt.

Colleen, having finally caught her ferocious enemy goose, looked as though she was about to wring its neck. Isabel's frazzled mother glanced around for help, causing Isabel to duck behind a table. Isabel prayed her mother had not seen her.

"Iz," her mother called. "I'm sure I saw you."

Isabel cursed under her breath. She loved her mother, but she simply did not have time to assist in saving her wedding decorations from an angst goose when she needed to solve a murder. As Colleen's shrill voice drew closer, interrupted by savage protesting quacks from the severely upset bird, Isabel panicked and scrambled under the peach tablecloth.

She soon discovered she was not alone under the table. A swish of leopard organza alerted her to Debbie. Debbie's long, muscular legs stuck out from a slit in her dress, and she grinned at Isabel.

"What are you doing here?" Isabel hissed at Debbie.

"The same thing you're doing. Hiding from your mother!"

"Are you sure it's not the police you're hiding from?" Isabel accused with a scowl.

"Me?" she spluttered. "Why would I have a reason to kill Micky?"

"You tell me. It seems most of the women attending this wedding were at some time or another involved with him. Were you?"

"How dare you!" Debbie spat at her, before pulling a cigarette out of her purse and lighting it. "My private life has nothing to do with you."

"But it has to do with this case. Every guest will be asked the same question, so you might as well tell me," Isabel said before choking on secondhand smoke and letting out a cough.

"I know you're here!" her mother called from a distance away.

Isabel fought back more coughing, which caused her eyes to water. She stared Debbie down.

Debbie narrowed her eyes on Isabel while she thought of a way to escape. She fluttered heavy, false eyelashes and then sighed. "Fine," she resigned with a dramatic wave of her cigarette hand, "Micky and I had a fling in our youth, once or twice, but nothing serious, and certainly nothing memorable."

"That explains why you were still flirting with him at the wedding."

"Darling," Debbie said in her husky, cigarette destroyed voice, "I flirt with any man I encounter, including your Ricardo."

Isabel refused to take the bait. She swallowed and kept her cool.

"Why did you crash my wedding?" Isabel asked directly. "We did not invite you. Your being here makes you a suspect."

"It hurt me that you didn't invite me," Debbie replied with a huff of smoke. "After all I've done for your art studio," she sniffed.

Isabel was stuck on trying to think about what Debbie had possibly done for her art studio.

"I've always loved your classes, and I felt as though we had a genuine bond. You taught me how to draw, and I helped you bring a little life," she flourished her hand like a Spanish dancer, almost setting the tablecloth on fire, "to your boring art lessons."

Isabel bit her tongue. Debbie was one of the most self-centered people she had ever met, which meant she was entirely oblivious to the feelings of others. Of course, a person like her would crash a wedding they had not been invited to, because what would a wedding be without her?

Isabel sighed, weary of the petty emotions that seemed behind most of the antagonism apparent among her guests.

"Did you know Micky was going to be here today?" Isabel asked, deciding it best to get back to the investigation.

Debbie snorted with laughter, "No, little Miss Nancy Drew, I didn't know a man I had a fling with, close on thirty years ago, was going to be here today."

"Did you speak to Micky at all after you separated?"

Debbie shook her head. "Even if we did, I wouldn't remember. He wasn't in my life for very long."

"I see," Isabel replied, not understanding what Debbie meant by that. "Apparently, Micky was briefly married to a woman with child. Did he ever mention that to you? It would have been around twenty-nine years ago."

Debbie twirled a red painted fingernail through her hair extensions. "I can't recall. The timing is close to me, but that was the thing with Micky. He often had a few girls going at the same time. Sorry, I can't be much help."

"Do you know of anyone who would have a motive to kill him?"

Debbie shrugged again, her shoulders barely moving in the cramped space under the table. Isabel was ready to pass out with the heavy odor of Debbie's perfume mingled with the oppressive cigarette smoke that burned her nose and throat.

"Thanks for your help." Isabel prepared to leave but paused. "You do bring a certain… passion to the art classes."

Debbie looked almost thankful, her wrinkled face relaxing as she looked at Isabel.

"I knew it!" a jarring shriek alarmed them both. "Hiding like a pair of naughty brats under the table!"

Isabel sighed as the protective tablecloth was wrenched from above, exposing their cramped hiding place.

"Mom, we were just talking and needed somewhere private," Isabel explained the second she crawled out from under the table. "Wait, what happened to you?"

Colleen was drenched from head to toe, her bright yellow dress shredded in parts. Her arms and hands bore red bruises as though she had been pinched repeatedly. Isabel looked over her mother's shoulder at a poor waiter trying to usher a flock of dreadfully irate geese back into their pen.

"Those savage beasts attacked me!" Colleen exploded with fury. "I was trying to rescue your wedding cakes from them, when they turned on me."

Isabel forced herself not to laugh outrageously at the emphasis Colleen placed on *them* as though the geese were a highly intelligent species that threatened to eradicate humanity.

"I'm sorry I didn't help," Isabel said sincerely. "Let's get those bite marks cleaned up. I'm sure Delta has something you can wear that's dry."

"Izzie, dear," her mother paused suddenly. "I remembered one of those thingies that could help you solve the case."

"A clue?" Isabel replied to her dazed mother. The over excitement of warring with the geese had gotten to her head.

"Yes," Colleen snapped her fingers. "I ordered everyone to place their gifts on a specific table in the sunroom. While you were making your way down to the ceremony, I saw a young woman snooping around the gifts."

"Which young woman?"

"The beautiful one that Ricardo's friend arrived with. The one in the tight dress."

"Pedro's date?" Isabel asked, her mind reeling.

"That's the one. He's a handsome lad, but she had wandering eyes. She was always looking around with shifty eyes which I found strange, since she was there with a delicious date."

Isabel ignored her mother's description of someone her age as a 'delicious date.'

"I don't even know her name. Pedro replied saying he would attend solo, so we weren't expecting him to arrive with a date. Thanks Mom, I'll look into it," Isabel smiled.

There was no response from Colleen. Her mother had suffered too many shocks for one day and had fainted on the grass. Debbie charged up in a flap of leopard print and helped Isabel drag her mother back to her feet.

Chapter 7
The Bumbling Bartender

"So, they didn't arrest you?" the striking woman asked, her hand sweeping a dark wave of hair over her shoulder.

"Well, no, but I can't exactly leave town either," Pedro grumbled, his drink inches from his twitching fingers. He sat slumped at the bar, brooding over his drink.

"But they found the cinnamon used to kill Micky in *your* gift bag," the woman pressed. "Isn't it automatic that they arrest you?"

Pedro raised a dark eyebrow and studied her. "You seem disappointed, Kittie, that your date isn't sitting behind bars for murder."

Kittie giggled playfully, her fingers stroking her silky hair. "Of course not," she assured him. "I've just always been interested in how police cases work. I thought it was as simple as, find the murder weapon and arrest the criminal. Case closed."

"I've never exactly heard cinnamon described as a murder weapon," Pedro mumbled without the slightest trace of humor. "And usually, the real killer plants his weapon on someone else. So, what everybody should really ask is who framed me?"

He drained his glass and tapped his fingers impatiently on the bar to signal the bartender to refill his drink. She jumped to it quickly, sloshing tequila on the counter.

Pedro stared at his glass as though it were a snake. "I was drinking whiskey," he pointed out with a touch of annoyance creeping into his voice. "I now have a glass filled with cheap tequila."

The flustered bartender jumped round to study the shelf of colorful bottles behind her. She could not see much under the hat she had pulled down low over her eyes.

"It's that one." Pedro pointed to the section of expensive whiskey bottles on the left.

The bartender poured him a full glass before clanking the bottle clumsily back on its shelf.

"I think I'll need a beer to wash this much down," Pedro added, as he dubiously watched the bartender fumble about her work.

"I'll have another gin and tonic," Kittie demanded, clearly tiring of the bartender's sluggishness.

The bartender busied herself with finding the drinks, her lips muttering the different brands of alcohol as though they were in a foreign language. A few lemons rolled across the floor and there was the sound of a chopping knife slamming into the board, followed by a muffled cry of pain.

"If you're so convinced someone is trying to frame you, then who do you think could have placed the cinnamon in your gift bag?" Kittie continued in her bored voice, while tapping impatiently on the counter.

"I do not know," Pedro shrugged. "I didn't even know Micky. I think that's what they called him. So why would I want to kill him? Someone is clearly trying to misdirect the detectives by providing me as a dead-end lead."

"Perhaps the killer didn't choose you as a target, but threw the cinnamon in there out of sheer desperation," the bartender interrupted, with a wad of bloody paper towel wrapped round her finger. "Here's your drink."

"Excuse me?" Kittie thrashed at her while snatching the glass off the counter. "This is a private conversation. You're paid to pour drinks, not eavesdrop, though you're failing miserably at that too."

"What do you mean by that?" Pedro asked the panicky bartender, who refused to make eye contact with either of them.

The bartender nearly dropped the gin bottle as she returned it to the shelf.

"What is this?" Kittie snapped, frowning at her drink, which had about five strawberries and half a lemon chopped up into it. "A fruit salad? I asked for gin."

"I thought berries went with gin," the bartender stammered uncertainly. "That's what google said."

Pedro snorted with laughter into the crook of his elbow, disguising it fairly well at first, but then booming with laughter. "Give her a break, Kittie. It's probably her first day on the job. Now tell us your theory about how the cinnamon got into my gift bag. You seem to be one of the few people here with a good head on your shoulders."

"I think the killer needed to get rid of evidence quickly. So, he, or *she,* dumped it into the first gift bag in sight. Possibly even because they didn't have their own gift bag to hide it in, like someone who didn't know the bride or groom at all."

"What do you mean by that?" Pedro asked, a crease appearing between his eyes.

"I think the real question is, Pedro, how well do you know your date?"

The question stunned Pedro. He scratched at the stubble on his chin, his mind turning over a thousand revolutions a second.

"Hey!" Kittie complained, a snarl forming across her perfectly pink lips. "What kind of bartender are you? I'm going to have you reported!"

"To whom?" the bartender inquired with a devious smile forming.

Kittie gave her a blank stare before finally responding, "The bride and groom!"

The bartender pulled her hat from her head, revealing long blonde hair and warm brown eyes that danced with elation.

"I am the bride."

"Isabel?" Pedro stumbled over her name, his surly face breaking out into a warm smile. "I can't believe I didn't know it was you. You never drink and you're clueless with alcohol in any form!"

Isabel bowed slightly, proud her little act fooled Pedro. "Yes, I thought it was one of my poorer disguises, but you fell for it regardless, so I might just use 'the bumbling bartender' in a future case."

"Would someone care to explain what the heck is going on here?" Kittie demanded after thumping her glass of strawberries on the table.

"I'm helping the police investigate Micky's murder. And I suspect you had something to do with it," Isabel stated confidently. "Your being here is no accident."

"Me?" Kittie exploded with a rather convincing shock.

Pedro chuckled. "Look, Iz. I arrived in town a couple of nights early. I didn't want to trouble you guys for a place to stay, because I figured you had a ton of wedding stuff to attend to. So, I stayed in a hotel and hit a few of the local bars to keep myself busy."

"That's where he met me. I was staying at the same hotel, and I bought him a drink," Kittie continued the story. "I'm from out of town, too. It was just a casual encounter. I enjoyed his company, and he enjoyed mine. So, naturally Pedro ended up inviting me to your wedding as his date."

"Well," Pedro interrupted, "you claimed you 'absolutely adored weddings and just had to come along,'" Pedro quoted in a high-pitched voice that was likely in imitation of a slightly tipsy Kittie.

She glared at him. "Well, I thought it would be fun. I didn't know someone was going to get murdered, and I'd end up in the middle of a police investigation."

"Why were you in Cyprus Cove?" Isabel asked, her sudden question catching Kittie off guard.

Kittie opened and closed her mouth a few times, as though she was trying to remember her story.

"There was an art exhibition I was interested in seeing," she managed.

"Oh, really? Which one?"

"I believe there is a… Picasso painting that is going to be exhibited at the local gallery in Cyprus Cove. I'm not sure when though."

"How exciting," Isabel chimed. "Well, let me get rid of this," Isabel smiled as she removed the glass of strawberries with a dash of gin, "and I'll send the real bartender back to you."

She could feel Pedro's eyes on her as she bolted away, carrying the glass carefully between the paper towels she had used to cover her fake injury. There were definite footsteps crunching behind her on the grass and, as she turned round to see who was following her, she spotted Pedro.

"I know what you're up to," he accused her, his eyes flicking to the strawberry filled glass in her hands.

"I didn't want to see the strawberries go to waste," Isabel stammered.

"You're a worse liar than Kittie is. Let's get her fingerprints to Rachel to run through the system. I want to know who my surprise date is just as much as you do."

***

Kittie, or Katrina Deborah Silva, had hoisted her rather tight cocktail dress up to her thighs. She kicked her heels off and tore a piece from her dress to tie up her mane of hair. After stealthily surveilling the area, which confirmed there were no unwelcome eyes watching her, Katrina leapt onto the towering wall and grappled her way up. She poked her toes into tiny crevices and pulled her body up, using the thick vines that clung to the walls like leafy spider webs.

There was a tense moment when one vine snapped and Katrina nearly fell backwards, but after sliding down a few feet, bruising and scraping every inch of her legs and arms, she clawed onto a stronger vine. With shaking arms and knees, Katrina hauled her trembling body back up and onto the top of the wall. She lay there, exhausted and panting, while she contemplated climbing down the other side and limping away to freedom.

She took a deep breath, sat up, and steadied herself with her filthy hands while she peered over the other side to scout out a good route down. Katrina carefully lowered herself over the edge of the wall, her toes feeling around for the tiniest of foot holds to support her weight. It was not a graceful descent, but she finally thumped bare feet into soft soil at the base of the wall. Elegance had not been Katrina's goal. She simply needed to get away undetected because the pesky bride, and apparent sleuth, had been asking far too many personal questions.

"Going somewhere?" Isabel's voice sounded again, lilting at the end to indicate she had asked yet another question.

Katrina jumped, her back slamming into the wall behind her, causing several frantic lizards to scatter and deposit dried leaves on her head.

"You!" Katrina shrieked in disbelief. "What are you doing here?"

"Oh, it's not just me," Isabel smirked. "I brought along some friends who'd like to meet you too."

Rachel and several uniformed officers stepped out from behind various hiding spots in the street. Rachel stepped forward. She had managed the entire investigation in her gown and high heels.

"I could've jumped this wall without destroying my dress and shoes," Rachel commented dryly after surveying the ragged Katrina covered in tears and scratches.

"Care to offer your version of why you were trying to escape being caught for murder?" Isabel asked triumphantly.

"I was trying to escape, but only because I was tired of being harassed by you people for a crime I *didn't* commit! And besides, I have an exhibition to get to."

"There's no exhibition. I'm on the committee that curates the exhibitions that feature at the gallery," Isabel explained smugly. "You're clearly lying. I have a different theory for why you're in town, Katrina Deborah Silva."

Katrina's jaw dropped at hearing her full name. She scowled ferociously at Isabel. "You stole my glass and lifted my prints! That's illegal!"

"Not when you're not an actual policeman," Isabel grinned. "I was just concerned about an uninvited person arriving at my wedding and had the police run your prints."

"My name proves nothing," Katrina spat.

"It proves something when your records show you changed your last name to Silva after your parents got divorced. It seems you refused to take either of their last names."

Katrina's eyes widened with fright, as though her darkest secret had been uncovered.

"Micky Robson was your father," Isabel stated boldly. "He abandoned you and your mother and so you came here to get revenge. You killed him."

"No," Katrina shook her head, fear paralyzing her. "There's been a mistake."

Rachel stepped up and yanked Katrina's clutch purse out from under the sleeve of her dress. She had stashed it there for safe keeping before the climb.

"That's mine!" Katrina objected weakly.

"You're an official suspect in a murder investigation. We may search items you're carrying with you," Rachel informed her professionally.

A quick flick through her purse revealed an old and worn photograph of Micky, along with a printout of his personal details. His name, address, and a conversation between him and Rosemary about the wedding had been transcribed on paper.

"Wait, please, there's been a misunderstanding," Katrina begged as an officer snapped a pair of handcuffs on her.

"'Allergies,'" Rachel was reading, "'cinnamon!'"

"I didn't even read that part!" Katrina objected loudly as she tried to thrash against the policemen, trying to arrest her. "I just wanted to talk to him."

"I think we've heard enough," Rachel said dismissively. "Let's get her to the interrogation room and begin formal questioning. I think we're all looking forward to leaving this wedding early."

"Wait, what did you want to talk to Micky about?" Isabel asked so that only Katrina could hear her.

Katrina turned wild, brown eyes on her, her face twisted with fear and panic.

"I just wanted to meet my father," Katrina cried in a hoarse voice as a policeman yanked her away. "Why would I kill him?"

"That's what all killers say," Rachel replied dryly.

Chapter 8
Talking Sideboards

"Your hotel record shows you've been in Cyprus Cove for around two weeks. Your credit card bills indicate you spent almost every night in bars chatting up anyone interested. Why?"

Rachel and Katrina were seated inside Delta's in-home modest-sized conference room. There was an impressively large sideboard that housed a coffee machine and a generous assortment of imported coffee beans. The outfacing wall was made of glass, revealing an elevated view of the ocean which stretched out vast and black in the night. The wave crests reflected white in the moonlight. Rachel ignored the view, her eyes fixed solely on Katrina.

"I was on vacation -" Katrina began.

Her posture no longer portrayed a confident young woman in her late twenties who believed she could attract any man with an alluring smile and charm him into doing her bidding. She clutched the police jacket around her shredded dress and her arms wrapped protectively round her.

Rachel arched a fierce eyebrow, signifying that she could tell when a suspect was lying. She slurped at her fifth cup of Italian coffee, her eyes never leaving Katrina the entire time.

"Alright," Katrina sighed in frustration, "I came here trying to track down my father."

"Why not just go to him directly?" a voice sounded from inside the sideboard.

Katrina scowled at the sideboard. "Is there someone in there?"

"Just answer the question," Rachel ordered with a roll of her eyes.

"Uh… okay, well, I didn't go to him directly because I couldn't find him. I heard he had gone on a boating trip. Which is why I ended up waiting in town for two weeks."

"He arrived the day before the wedding. Why not approach him then?" the sideboard asked.

Katrina gestured in protest at the talking sideboard, but Rachel simply shook her head and closed her eyes. The silence stretched on awkwardly until Katrina finally buckled and answered the sideboard.

"Well, I lost my nerve, to be honest. Approaching a man who walked out on you when you were two and left your mother an emotional mess… it's not as easy as you think," she responded defensively. "So, I tried to think of another way to observe him from a safe distance first, you know, to see the kind of person he is… was…"

"Is that why you deceived Pedro into bringing you to the wedding as his date?" Rachel inquired.

"There was no deception. I expressed how much I loved weddings and he invited me."

"But you had an ulterior motive," Rachel added.

"Yes, to see Micky, but not to kill him."

"Then why were you trying to pin the murder on Pedro?" the sideboard added. "You were asking him all those questions at the bar."

Katrina scowled again. "I was questioning Pedro because I wanted to figure out who killed Micky just as much as you people."

"Tell us about your mother," the sideboard changed the subject.

"Look, I'm not answering any more questions from the talking sideboard."

Rachel sighed. "It's a little problem we have in the Cyprus Cove police department," she explained in a low voice, glancing over her shoulder at the sideboard. "While we might be tremendously capable detectives who feel we can do our jobs proficiently, we also have a valuable addition to our task force, whether or not we like it."

Katrina looked even more confused.

"Come out, Isabel. You may as well just join the interrogation if you will not stay hidden and allow *me* to conduct the interview."

A cupboard in the sideboard creaked open and Isabel unfolded limb by limb before crawling out.

"I thought you were doing just fine," Isabel remarked to the surly detective. "You just weren't quite hitting the questions I needed you to. Katrina, tell us about your second name."

"Deborah?"

"That's the one."

"It's my mother's name."

"I know," Isabel said with a smile. "What I don't understand is why you pretended your own mother didn't exist even though you've both spent the last several hours together at my wedding."

Katrina dropped her gaze to the tabletop in front of her, her fingers twitching nervously.

"My mother and I aren't exactly close."

"That much is obvious," Rachel remarked.

"When Micky left, I was stuck home with Mom. Things were alright I guess, but Mom was always desperate for attention. She would leave me for hours on end while she frequented bars. Let's just say she never came home alone."

"That couldn't have been an easy life for you growing up," Isabel sympathized.

Isabel felt a twinge of guilt at how casually she had dismissed her mother's love as oppressive. Colleen and Violet were many things, but Isabel could never accuse either of them of not loving her and doing everything in their power for her. Another stab of guilt ripped through her when she thought of the wedding dress she had torn off, with no feeling for her mother.

"No," Katrina replied with an edge of hostility in her voice. "It was terrible, especially when my mom passed out and…" she drifted off. "I left when I was fourteen and bounced around between various aunts and uncles. I never looked back."

"What made you want to seek Micky then?"

"I wanted to know why he ruined our lives. I blame him for what happened to my mother," Katrina explained glumly.

"I just felt that I needed some kind of explanation before I could move on with my life. And now I'll never get that."

"Yeah, because you killed him," Rachel replied bluntly.

"I didn't kill him!"

"Did your mother know you were trying to attend the wedding?"

"Yes," Katrina admitted. "When I couldn't find out anything about Micky's whereabouts, I contacted my mother out of desperation. That's when I found out about the wedding and that one woman here would take Micky as a date."

"How did Debbie react?"

"She said she had forgiven him for ruining our lives and that I should, too. She also said that if I confronted him, it would likely just lead to me getting even more hurt. So, I guess you could say she wasn't pleased with the idea."

"Why do you think that was?"

"I think she was just trying to protect me. When I told her I still wanted to go through with it, she said she would attend your wedding too, so that she could keep an eye on us."

"Thanks for your honestly," Isabel said with a small smile. "Please excuse me."

"So, you break out of the sideboard, interrupt my investigation, and then just leave!" Rachel scolded her.

But Isabel had already darted out the door. She knew exactly who she needed to talk to next.

Chapter 9
Brawling With
a Leopard

"So," Isabel said loudly before pausing dramatically and waiting for the swish of leopard print fabric. "I met your daughter."

Debbie froze, her self-mixed martini poised in her hand. Isabel glimpsed the handsome bartender, clearly hiding away from the flirtatious reaches of Debbie. Isabel gave him the nod to disappear, and he clasped his hands gratefully at her before dashing away.

"And?" Debbie asked after composing herself.

"I thought it odd that you didn't really acknowledge her to all your friends. That's what you called us, remember. If you had enough courage to break into a wedding we did not invite you to, surely you'd be brave enough to tell us you had a daughter."

"I don't know what she was doing here. And besides, what business is it of yours?"

"Well, your daughter's father dropped dead this afternoon," Isabel explained the obvious connection. "And you failed to mention the connection to the police."

"For this very reason," Debbie replied. "I didn't want to waste police time appearing to be a suspect when, of course, I'm not."

Isabel found her eyebrow arching in much the same way Rachel had.

"Even when your own daughter was arrested," Isabel continued. "Surely that should've moved you to speak up, at least on her behalf."

"Well, how do I know she didn't kill Micky? That girl has always had it in for her father. And I don't blame her."

"That's not the same story I heard from Violet, Ricardo's mother."

Debbie rolled her eyes and snorted before draining her glass. "Violet is only a sore loser. If I recall right, Micky left her for me. Too bad I wasn't interested."

"Violet said that Micky left her to marry a woman who was pregnant with his child. Micky didn't know Violet was pregnant too. If I look at the ten-month age gap between Ricardo, Violet's son, and Katrina, your daughter, it's easy to figure out that you were the woman Micky offered marriage to."

"What's your point?" Debbie demanded while pouring herself another dry martini.

"There's no record of a marriage certificate between you and Micky."

Debbie turned slowly and smiled. "We didn't bother with one."

"I don't believe you. You paint Micky out to be this terrible man who refused to commit to you, but I don't see you as the type of woman wanting anyone to commit to her."

Debbie's eyes narrowed, giving her an almost snake-like appearance as she stepped closer to Isabel.

"So what?" Debbie blew the martini-flavored words in her face. "I told Micky I was pregnant and demanded he marry me because I knew he was with another woman. I thought the stupid man would offer me money to stay silent, not leave his girlfriend and drop on one knee."

"You never wanted marriage out of him… You wanted money. Which is probably why you got yourself pregnant."

"That's a bold accusation. Katrina was an accident."

"I don't think so," Isabel shook her head. "A woman as promiscuous as you has only produced one child, which means you know exactly how to take the right precautions to prevent unwanted pregnancies. But when the charming, wealthy Micky came along, you saw an opportunity to fund your lavish lifestyle and you made an exception."

"There's no crime in that," Debbie snarled at her. "I didn't come from money. I had to work hard for everything I have. I can see you look down on me and despise me for what I did, but how do you know you wouldn't do the same if you were in my shoes?"

"Because I was in your shoes. I left the comfort of home and arrived here with nothing. The difference between you and me is that I have made good friends, and they helped me through tough times. You turn your back on everyone, caring only about yourself, and your relentless pursuit of wealth has left you alone."

"Again, Isabel Austin, these are not actual crimes you are accusing me of," Debbie pointed out with an air of superiority, "so, if you'll excuse me, I need to gather my things to leave."

"What makes you think you're leaving?"

"Well, the killer has been caught, and your bar is running dry. What need is there for me to hang around?"

"Katrina is not the killer. She came here to talk to her father, and to gain some closure. She believes he ruined your life and hers."

"And?"

"And that's not the truth. He tried to do the right thing, but you rejected him."

Debbie fired a heated glare, her entire frame ridged with tension.

"You didn't want your daughter, or anyone else, to know that you're the actual person to blame for ruining her life and your own."

Debbie took her glass by the stem and smashed it on the bar counter. "Of course, I didn't want her to find out! Micky left Katrina a vast amount of money in an inheritance fund. And I know for a fact that despite Katrina not wanting anything to do with me, she still has me as the sole inheritor on her will. So, I couldn't allow her to find out the truth from Micky and have my income jeopardized!"

This had been more information than Isabel was aware of. She had simply been trying to prod Debbie into confessing something that would link her to the case. But Debbie had unknowingly admitted her private motive for murder. Her daughter's inheritance. Or had she done it knowingly?

Isabel glanced around. The garden was dark except for the few wavering garden lights and lanterns that had been set up for the reception. There were no staff members or guests floating around because everyone else was preparing to leave after the worst wedding they had ever attended. The garden was still, except for the remote flap of a bat or a moth fluttering against a light.

If Debbie had been smart enough to conjure a lifelong plan that would result in her inheriting a man's money without having to marry him, then she would certainly not be stupid enough to let her motive for murder slip out in a casual conversation with someone marrying the chief detective on Micky's murder case.

Isabel took a step back. Debbie was sneering at her, her lips smothered in deep red. A chill raked Isabel's spine, and she noticed the broken stem of glass in Debbie's hand. Debbie took another step closer.

"So, you planned Micky's murder. Were you the one who told him that his daughter would be at the wedding? Is that what lured him here?"

Debbie nodded smugly, clearly proud of her malevolent handiwork.

"You knew killing him would be as easy as a few shakes of a cinnamon shaker. With Micky out the way, you could go about framing Katrina."

"I knew the police would eventually figure out Katrina's connection to Micky and that would paint her in a suspicious light. If they also found the murder weapon in her date's gift bag, then everything would fall into place," Debbie explained confidently. "There was only one thing I didn't bank on."

"Me," Isabel stated flatly.

"Exactly," Debbie sneered, lipstick smearing onto her teeth. "Your idiot, interfering, snooping, and annoying self almost ruined everything. Why can't you just accept the clues?"

"Because the clues don't always match a person's heart. All the evidence is stacked against Katrina, but she doesn't have the heart of a killer. When given the chance to fight or run, she tried to escape over a wall. I believe she came here sincerely wanting answers from her father. But you knew that once Micky told her the truth, she would disinherit you. More motive to kill him and frame her. I suppose you planned to pay off someone in prison to get rid of her."

"I have a few friends on the inside, actually."

"It was your heart that gave you away," Isabel accused her. "I tried so hard to like you, but I watched you dominate every space you ever walked into, and always at the expense of those you considered weaker than you."

"The question is," Debbie said with a smirk as she advanced again, her fist tightening around the sharp stick of glass, "what are you going to do about it?"

"I'm going to have you arrested and sent to jail for the crime you committed."

Debbie laughed into the cool night air, her voice echoing slightly around the empty garden.

"How about I give you two choices?" Debbie offered her. "Number one, you continue to stand in my way, and I'll be forced to put an end to you like I did Micky. Or your second option. Let me escape and no one has to know it involved me. When Micky's money comes through, I'll give you a fair share for your help."

"What makes you think I would ever accept a bribe to hide the truth?"

"Because you're tired of being told what to do. I groaned inwardly when I saw that hideous dress and knew immediately you were probably only wearing it because your mom put it together for you. You've got zero backbone, and it's time you grew one. So do something for yourself for a change."

"You underestimate me," Isabel stated loudly, while throwing her shoulders back and standing tall. "I bend over for other people because I love them, and it makes me happy to see them happy."

"Now you're the one lying. You hated every second in that dress."

"Fine, I hated the dress! I hated the cake, the geese, and most of all, I hated the peach! But none of it really matters. I love the people I have in my life, and I'd rather have them with me than have whatever I want, but be entirely alone. Like you. I don't envy you. No one does. We pity you. Now give it up, you're going to jail."

Debbie clenched her jaw and lurched forward with unexpected speed for someone her age. Layers of floating leopard print fabric confused Isabel, which she tried to swipe away with her hands. Suddenly pain slashed through her side as something sharp pricked her skin. Isabel touched her fingers to her waist and felt the warm, sticky sensation of oozing blood.

For a split second, Debbie's eyes met hers. Debbie grinned and yanked backwards, pulling the glass from Isabel's side. Isabel shrieked with pain, dropping to her knees as life trickled out of her drop by drop.

"I warned you," Debbie sniggered into her ear. "That's not a fatal wound, so quit whimpering. I'm giving you one last chance to help me."

"I'll never help you get away with murder!" Isabel screamed, before Debbie silenced her with a slap.

"Then you're making me guilty of committing a second murder," Debbie hissed at her with a sinister shadow crossing her face in the dull light.

Isabel tried to squirm out of Debbie's perfumed grip. Her side was already on fire with pain, and she could feel her heart throbbing like a lump in her throat. She wanted to be sick, but also felt the creeping sensation of giving up to let Debbie finish her.

How differently Isabel's wedding had turned out from the one she had dreamed of. She wondered if everything would still have happened if they had just planned their wedding for the previous day. Micky would still be happily sailing the world on his boat, alive. Katrina would struggle with questions about her father, but at least she would not be facing a prison sentence. And Debbie would not be a murderer.

Debbie slowly raised the glass shard until Isabel could feel the stinging prick in her neck. She tried to stay calm and breathe, but the movement caused the glass to cut deeper into her throat.

Seconds passed, and in that time Isabel's mind warred between acceptance and refusal. She was young and strong and had fought hard to move forward in her life. She would not kneel at Debbie's feet. She would not allow Debbie to steal away her life, not without a fight.

"No," Isabel breathed painfully. The objection was more to herself giving up, than to Debbie inching deeper with her weapon.

Isabel wrenched an arm out of Debbie's grip and wrapped her fingers around Debbie's glass knife hand. She pushed with all her strength, the glass scraping across her neck as she did, but not cutting deeply enough to cause any actual harm.

Debbie glowered at her with stunned eyes. Isabel pushed the old woman away from her, realizing that no matter how much time Debbie had spent doing Pilates and pumping Botox, Isabel was stronger physically. She just needed to be stronger mentally.

"This is me standing up for myself and what I believe in," she yelled at Debbie, who had fallen to the ground some feet away. "You're a murderer and you deserve to be punished."

"Okay," Debbie sobbed, her face cowering behind her arm as though Isabel was going to strike her. She raised her arms and opened her hands in surrender. The bloody stem of glass rolled out and onto the grass. "I give up. I'll tell the police everything," she whimpered.

Isabel sighed in relief. She turned around, her hand clutching her side, to see if Ricardo or Rachel were within earshot and could help her arrest Debbie.

When she turned to face Debbie again, the old woman had disappeared.

"What?" Isabel gasped in shock, her eyes blinking hard at the dark shrubbery around her.

Blinding light flashed before Isabel's eyes, followed by impenetrable darkness, and the softness of grass blades tickling her cheek.

Chapter 10
Swimming With the Fishes

It had been a rookie mistake. Of course, Isabel did not recall this immediately after she opened her eyes. Instead, she was greeted with a splitting headache that seemed to reach into her skull and squeeze all the bones together.

She raised her head from the cold grass and winced at the pain that radiated from the cut in her side and the thudding bump on the back of her head. Slowly, vague images of Debbie wearing leopard print formed in her clouded brain. She tried to blink away the blurriness that obstructed her view, while her fingers inched over her icy skin to figure out where the pain was coming from. She felt the sticky blood at her side and remembered the sharp pain that had ripped through her when Debbie stabbed her with the glass.

Isabel groaned and tried to leap up from the grass. The sudden movement caused her head to spin, and a wave of nausea washed over her. Isabel turned and hurled the entire contents of her stomach into the bush. Debbie's perfume still lingered on some of the leaves, and another memory escaped Isabel's foggy mind the moment she tried to catch onto it.

Debbie was the killer. Isabel remembered figuring this out. Euphoria warmed her for a brief instant before she recalled Debbie's invisible escape.

"Izzie!" Ricardo smacked into her. "We've been searching for you for over an hour. We figured out who the killer is!"

"Debbie?" Isabel replied dryly.

"How could you have possibly figured that out already…" Ricardo's eyes seemed to see her for the first time as more torches lit up the severity of her appearance. "What happened to you?" Ricardo barked, his eyes filling with panic as he took in the stripe of blood round her neck.

"I'm fine," Isabel assured him. "They're mostly just surface scratches."

"You've got vomit on your shirt," Rachel, ever the observant detective, pointed out.

"Okay, so I'm not feeling exactly great, but I'm well enough to carry on without a medic," Isabel explained. "I confronted Debbie and things didn't go as planned."

"Oh my gosh," Ricardo roared, "you're bleeding! She stabbed you! Someone stabbed my bride!"

Ricardo looked as though he was going to be the next person to pass out. While he had zero trouble dealing with bloody scenes, as it was a prerequisite for the job, he had serious reservations about blood that belonged to his fiancé.

"Relax, Romeo," Rachel said sternly, her hand ringing against his cheek as she delivered a stinging slap.

"Thanks," Ricardo breathed again. "I think I needed that."

"Look, Debbie got away and we can't waste any more time worrying about me. Did you guys catch Debbie?" Isabel asked desperately. "She's far more dangerous than she looks and she's after money."

"No, by the time we got through all the paperwork, including Micky's will, and put it all together, Debbie was long gone," Rachel explained glumly.

"We've been combing this place, looking for her and you," Ricardo explained. "I was so worried," he babbled tearfully.

"Keep it together, man," Rachel warned him, her hand threatening to offer another wake-up slap.

This made it even more obvious why Ricardo had chosen his detective partner to be his best 'man' at his wedding. Rachel had a way of keeping a man calm who never seemed to lose his calm.

"Is Katrina safe?" Isabel asked quickly.

"Yes, she has a couple of officers with her at all times. She gave us her mother's address, and we sent a patrol car ahead of us, but there was no one there, though they said they had tossed the place up a bit."

Isabel thought for quite some time. Usually, she could snap the facts together as quickly as they had been presented to her, but with the growing concussion, increasing blood loss, and general adrenaline fatigue, Isabel was not herself.

"Any day now, Sherlock," Rachel fired at her, the anxiety clearly frazzling the rest of her patience.

"I think I know where she's going," Isabel finally managed, with a weak smile of triumph revitalizing her for the last hurdle. "Let's catch ourselves a killer."

***

It was long after midnight and the cool sea air brushed through her hair and gripped icy fingers around her neck. She felt as though the entire world was mere inches from hunting her down. She reminded herself that no one had followed her. She had crept soundlessly into the harbor, her hollow footsteps along the wooden jetties masked by the creaking and knocking of boats and yachts. The moonlight illuminated her path, reflecting on the black waters below and giving it the appearance of thick oil.

Things had certainly gotten a little messy at the wedding. Katrina was supposed to take the fall, especially with all the evidence so carefully positioned to point her way. The pesky, little, slimy sleuth, who hid under the guise of an innocent local artist, had ruined everything. Debbie fumed as she thought of the simplicity of her brilliant plan, undone in a matter of hours by Isabel Austin and her little friends. She regretted wasting time making Isabel a partnership offer when she should have just ended things there and then. But passing up a person as skilled and quick-thinking as Isabel had been too difficult to resist.

Debbie blew out her frustration and scrunched her eyes shut. She needed her brain calm and free to focus on her stored knowledge of sailing. There had been several boyfriends in the past that had owned boats and Debbie had made sure she had learned a thing or two, especially since she recalled stealing at least two of those boats.

She smiled grimly to herself in the darkness. What a life she had led. Often on the run until she could fool the next group of people into taking her in. Her life had been made up of an exhilarating series of decades. Her wrists ached sharply as she undid the knots holding down the sail. Her stiff fingers throbbed as she forced them to cooperate.

Her body was screaming its age at her, reminding her she was too old to survive on the run. There was no way she could operate such a big vessel on her own and successfully navigate out of the harbor on a breezy night, especially once she hit open water. There was a reason she had adopted a quieter way of life and settled in Cyprus Cove.

"Oh, shut up, you old fool," she rumbled at herself as she flicked away anxious tears. "You've gotten out of far worse! What's one more adventure!"

"I'm sure you have," a familiar voice sounded through the night air.

Debbie jumped in fright, her foot hooking on a loop of rope lying on the deck of Micky's boat. The more she tried to pull away, the more tangled in rope she ended up. Finally, without Isabel even having to touch her, Debbie's own panic imprisoned her in a web of rope.

"I knew I should've killed you when I had the chance!" Debbie hissed at her as she tried to scramble out of the trap. "Why do you have to keep interfering in matters that don't concern you!"

"You murdered someone at my wedding!" Isabel snapped back at her. "And to make it worse, Micky was my groom's biological father, who, I suspect, only came to the wedding to see his son get married. This completely concerns me in every way!"

Debbie rolled her eyes. "So what if I murdered Micky? The police have Katrina as their killer, thanks to me. Everyone wins."

"You're forgetting that this case concerns me too," Ricardo stated loudly as he stepped out of the darkness, the handcuffs on his hip clinking. He had his gun ready and aimed at Debbie.

Debbie struggled to get out of the loops of rope that had encircled her. Fear rippled through her eyes as Ricardo descended on her. After kicking away the last snakelike end of rope, Debbie backed away to the edge of the boat and offered a feral snarl.

"You're under arrest," Rachel began, a yawn escaping. "For the murder of -"

"You have no proof!" Debbie interrupted in a shrill voice that sent the sleeping seagulls squawking in panic.

"We have a confession, apart from anything else," Ricardo informed her. "Not only did you stab Isabel, but you confessed your murder to her earlier as well -"

"It's her word against mine," Debbie interrupted fiercely. Her hands had gripped the railing of the boat and she looked ready to launch herself over the side at any moment. "I saw her trip and land on the glass she was carrying."

"But," Ricardo spoke over her, "seconds ago, you also confessed in the presence of two police detectives," Ricardo concluded while gesturing to Rachel, who wore a smug smirk.

"It's over," Isabel breathed.

"Like he was saying, you're under arrest," Rachel repeated. She pulled out her own set of handcuffs, which had been conveniently velcro-ed to her upper leg, and approached the old woman with a smug smile.

"There's nowhere to run," Isabel reminded her. "Surely, even you have to be tired of constantly hiding from your problems. It's time to stop and face the consequences of everything you've done."

Debbie glanced over her shoulder as though she was contemplating whether she would make the dive into the dark water below, or crash into the neighboring boat.

Rachel reached out a hand to grab Debbie, but the old woman still had some fight in her. She clasped onto Rachel's hand with both of her own and yanked the unsuspecting detective forward. Rachel, who had in no way been expecting retaliation of any kind, lost her footing in the bundles of rope at her feet and plummeted face first over the railing.

A splash from below indicated Rachel had made the jump to the water, rather than painfully, and possibly fatally, face planting on a jetty.

Ricardo lurched forward, but Debbie was smart and took her chances running down an already wounded Isabel. Isabel would not repeat the mistake of underestimating Debbie's strength, and so she braced herself against the impact. In the last moment, Isabel stepped out of the way and hooked a piece of rope with her foot, pulling it taut.

Debbie's foot caught. The top part of her body kept moving while her feet stayed behind. Isabel winced as she sent an old lady crashing to the hard deck, but she consoled herself with the fact that the same old woman had murdered an innocent man and attempted to do the same to her.

Ricardo slapped handcuffs on Debbie and helped her carefully to her feet. He did a once over to make sure she was okay. Isabel had seen him be far less gentle with other murders once he had caught them, but Debbie's 'old lady' act had been an asset in helping her escape suspicion for years.

"That old hag!" a peeved Rachel screamed below from the icy waters.

Isabel hurried to the railing and in the dull grey light of early morning, she saw Rachel swimming furiously to the edge of the jetty where she shoved a few sleepy sea gulls out the way so that she could haul herself out of the water.

"It's over," Isabel breathed in relief, tears of joy springing to her eyes. She grimaced with pain from her side, and her head started thumping as though all the adrenaline that had been keeping her going depleted the instant Debbie was captured.

"Izzie?" a concerned voice pierced through the cloudiness of her thoughts.

The voice seemed so distant. Isabel turned slowly to see Ricardo walking closer towards her, but the light was fading again, descending everything into the darkest of night, again. As her cheek hit cold, hard wood, Isabel sighed and closed her eyes.

Chapter 11
The Barefoot Bride

Isabel emptied her lungs of air, the deep exhalation blowing up the hair around her forehead and revealing the yellowed bruise Debbie had left her with. She dabbed a thin layer of foundation over the bruise and stepped back to see if it was still visible.

"One almost wouldn't believe that a week ago you'd been attacked by your fiancée's father's killer, and ex-girlfriend. Did I get that right?"

Isabel chuckled. Once she had put some space between her and the catastrophic failure that had been her wedding, Isabel could think on it without bursting into tears or trembling from head to foot.

"It still feels like a nightmare that didn't really happen to me," Isabel admitted quietly, her face growing serious.

"But it did. That's why your father and I have some news to share."

Isabel braced herself for the worst.

"We're going to move to Cyprus Cove."

"Mom!" Isabel squealed.

"I know, I know," her mother waved her down. "You don't want your old parents driving you insane and interfering with your life. I get that now. You're more than capable of taking care of yourself, and somehow seem to survive even when an insane, old woman tried," her voice wobbled, "to stab you with a piece of her martini glass... Oh Izzie!"

"It's okay, Mom, really," Isabel said, stroking her mother's arm with her hand.

"We're moving here to be closer to you, but also because we've really grown to love this little town. And I think I could almost see myself getting along with Ricardo's mother."

"That's very big of you," Isabel commended her mother. "I wanted to say that I love the idea. In the past, I wanted nothing more than to run away from you all, but now I realize the value of knowing who your family is and being close to them at all times. Ricardo, Katrina... they don't know what it's like to come from a stable, loving home like I do. I will always be grateful for what you and Dad have given me."

"But," her mother hesitated, her eyes flicking to the armchair where the plastic covering of a dress lay draped, "you won't reconsider wearing a wedding dress from me... when the time comes?"

Isabel shifted her weight uncomfortably, her eyes darting away from her mother's penetrating and all-knowing stare. The guilt of the lie had been hanging heavily over her, but she had not found the right time to bring it up.

"There's something I have to tell you about the old dress you made me. I was the one who ripped myself out of it. I'm so sorry, I feel terrible about lying to you, but the honest truth, from the beginning, was that I hated the dress. I just didn't want to hurt your feelings!"

Her mother chortled with cheerful laughter rather than shrieked with rage. "I know dear, I realized that a long time ago. I shouldn't have pushed my way on you. To make up for it, I bought you a dress for the breakfast picnic this morning. Delta and Rosemary helped me choose it, so I think you'll approve. It's far more appropriate than the denim shorts and t-shirt thing you've got going. And would it kill you to put some make-up on? Ricardo and his mother are going to be there."

Isabel shrugged. "It's just a beach picnic." As she said this, she noticed her mother's own dressed up appearance and sensed something was up.

Colleen fired a fierce scowl at her highly intelligent and talented daughter, amazed at how dense she was being.

"Isabel Mae Austin," her mother ordered, "put on the dress, now!"

Isabel jolted in fright. She was used to being ordered around by her mother, but this had been on an entirely different level of intensity. Finally, she stepped over to the dress bag and unzipped it, her breath catching in her throat when she saw what it contained.

* * *

It was a perfect morning. The sunlight danced through the palm fronds and warmed the beach sand. Isabel could smell the perfumed frangipanis and vanilla scented candles which lined out the aisle for her to walk along to her waiting groom. Isabel smiled as her bare feet sank into golden beach sand.

The small audience turned to watch her approach. Rosemary, Delta, Pedro, Thomas, Violet, her parents, and a few others she had been close to smiled at her as she made her way, step by step and in time to some distant ukulele tune, down the aisle. She noticed with a smile that all her guests were barefoot too.

It was the perfect moment. Exactly what she had wished to have on her wedding day. The beauty of the ocean reaching out endlessly in front of her. The warmth and sincerity lining the faces of a few intimate guests. And, most importantly, the man she loved waiting at the end of her short journey, ready to make her his wife.

As her eyes locked with Ricardo's, she realized none of it mattered. Peach bows, rabid geese, hideous wedding dresses, and the occasional murder. It was all completely and utterly unimportant when compared to the honor she now possessed of marrying the man she loved with all her heart.

As Ricardo took her hand in his, his warm fingers squeezing hers with gentle reassurance, Isabel wondered at the immense future that lay ahead of them. One filled with many more art works, murder mysteries, late night investigations, dinners with the in-laws, and a lifetime together.

The End

Now that you have finished this cozy mystery, please consider posting a review on Amazon. It would be appreciated.